The Asshole Conspiracy

*Is There Time
To Stop It?*

by Xavier Crement, M.D.

ENTHEA PRESS
Atlanta, Georgia

The Asshole Conspiracy

Life is not the same as it once was. It used to be filled with simple pleasures. Now it seems to be filled with multiple irritations:

- MTV.
- Government by special interests.
- Shrill claims of "sexual harassment."
- A trillion dollar national debt.
- Illiteracy in our public schools.
- Political correctness.
- More people on the dole than a payroll.

Who decided that these things were okay? Not us. Was it you?

Or was it a conspiracy of assholes?

—Angus Tailhook
Near Rear Admiral, USN
Retired

The Asshole Trilogy:

Asshole No More

Assholes Forever

The Asshole Conspiracy

None of the names used in this book are the names of actual living people, except in the cases of a few mega-assholes, but if you can't figure out who we are referring to, you need to start reading the papers more.

If you are offended by the contents of this book, or any part of it, you are probably an asshole. If you want to stop being an asshole, please sign up for Dr. Crement's therapy. If you are comfortable being an asshole, please buy a few dozen copies of this book and pass them out to the few friends and acquaintances you have left. They will need it.

The views expressed in this book are not necessarily the views of the publisher. But he thinks they are.

We are an equal opportunity offender.

Table of Contents

Introduction

"It stinks," Joe whispered. He was
right.

I woke up in the middle of the night, sweating bullets. It was stormy outside, and not much better on the inside. I had just been having a horrible dream.

A herd of brown donkeys had invaded a valley in which I and my comrades had been peacefully grazing. I was a cow—a contented one, too. But then the donkeys came. They ate all our forage. They terrorized the herd. They broke all the rules. They sowed seeds of division. They defecated everywhere. Then they moved on, to do the same thing elsewhere.

Normally, a dream of this nature would not have unduly disturbed me. But this was the tenth night in a row it had repeated itself. I wasn't getting any sleep. I was tired of being hassled by the jackasses. And, besides, my milk had gone sour.

So I stayed up to interpret it. Having spent years overcoming my own innate tendencies toward assholism, and years more helping other assholes reform themselves, the interpretation was not too difficult. The assholes were coming—and it wasn't going to be pleasant.

But who? And how?

I thought immediately of my brother-in-law, one of the most obnoxious flaming assholes I have ever endured—and insufferable, too, since he always ridicules the work I have done. Perhaps my dream was warning me that he was coming for a stay.

I ruled that out, however—it was a group of donkeys, not just one mammoth jackass.

Or perhaps the end of the world was indeed coming, as is so often predicted just before a millenium. The herd of donkeys annihilated our food supply and poisoned our water. But then I realized that even though that might be the end of the world for us cows, it obviously wasn't the end of anything for the jackasses. They had simply moved on, to begin a new cycle of pillage and destruction.

The thought passed fleetingly through my mind that perhaps the donkeys represented assholes in society, but I didn't pay much attention to it. After all, as the world's leading authority on assholism, I have become a champion of helping assholes become decent human beings. Over the years, I have been a midwife in the transformation of thousands and thousands of assholes into loving, kind, and gentle people. I know that goodwill works. So I was not yet prepared to embrace the possibility that assholism might be becoming stronger, rather than weaker—that it might be undermining the very pillars and posts of society.

After all, my first two books have become runaway bestsellers, even though they have been ignored by both the print and electronic media. They have been read by millions of people—folks I could never have possibly reached through my classes or consultations.

I first described the disease of assholism in my landmark report, *Asshole No More*. This book described the characteristics of assholism and how it could be cured. It was followed by my second book, *Assholes Forever,* in which I reported my discovery that certain people are confirmed assholes— like my brother-in-law—and are beyond treatment. The best way to handle them is to exclude them from your life as much as possible.

These two books popularized the problem of assholism and led to the formation of thousands of ANAL (Asshole Non-Anonymous Leagues) support groups throughout the world. They meet every week to help themselves and other recovering assholes confront the truth about themselves:

"My name is Dave, and I am an asshole."

Some people, by the way, wonder why I use the term "asshole." Isn't it an example of frightful manners? Of course it is. But that is precisely the point. Assholes are people who do not play by the rules of society. Before you can help them, you have to shock them out of their smug complacency. If you call them victims, they will continue to play that role. If you call them bullies, they will thank you. But if you call them "assholes," some of them will wake up and begin to smell the truth about their lives. It is the first step toward recovery.

I am proud of the work I have done and the service I have performed, not only on behalf of the assholes of the world, but even more importantly, for those who have suffered from them. It is true that I have been treated like a pariah by my fellow psychiatrists, but it is only because they are still assholes and know it. They resent the fact that I have exposed their hypocrisy.

Were they the donkeys, I wondered? No, I concluded, because envy is green, not brown, and it tends to consume the person who is jealous, not his or her target.

Intuitively, though, I sensed that I was honing in on the truth. My mind flashed back to a recent talk show on which I had appeared. The host had also invited the author of a book debunking my ideas on assholism, Phœnecia Iland, to appear. Her book is entitled *Exposing the Whole Asshole Myth*. She contends that assholism is not only innate in humanity but a desirable trait, in that it has allowed men and women to survive.

As I had suspected, Phœnecia tried hard to discredit me, asking one shit-trench question after another—questions which, no matter how you answer them, tend to leave you covered in crap. But ultimately, she just revealed her own inadequate understanding of the subject.

After the show, even though I knew I had scored a major victory, I was troubled. The pieces of the puzzle still were not coming together.

When I first realized that I was an asshole, the revelation was like a breath of fresh air that purged my life. In point of fact, it did change my life. But now that I have shared this revelation with the rest of humanity—and given them the tools to recover— why do we seem to be losing the battle? There are more decent human beings on the face of the earth than ever before, but the assholes still seem in control—and growing stronger.

In the back of my mind, I heard the rumbling of the donkeys once more. I must be getting close to the truth.

And then I knew. Naïvely, I had assumed that my efforts would inspire all decent human beings to come together and unite in the struggle against assholism. But it wasn't happening. The decent human beings were too decent to unite and become a dominant force. They forgave the assholes and accepted them with tolerance. And the assholes were taking advantage of the situation.

"They are gaining on us," I muttered. "This cannot be a fluke. They must be organized." With my trained eye, I spotted the signs of it immediately.

Assholes, of course, have always been with us. The mere appearance of war, strife, conflict, and divisiveness in society is no clear sign that assholes are organizing. After all, it only takes one bully asshole to turn an efficient office into a shambles; just one sissy-sweet asshole to turn a loving family into a breeding pit of hatred and competitiveness. In fact, I often use the "just one" model of analysis in my lectures, to encourage my listeners to strengthen their decent human character traits.

"It takes just one asshole to ruin your Sunday afternoon drive. But it only takes one decent human being—you—to stop reacting to the asshole.

"It takes just one asshole to sabotage your promotion at work. But it only takes one decent human being—you—to outperform the asshole and win in the end.

"It takes just one asshole parent to traumatize

you as a child. But it only takes one decent human being—you—to grow up and forgive these abuses once you are an adult."

As I tried to understand my dream, however, I knew that we were up against more than just a bunch of free-lance assholes. How did I figure it out? The answer came to me while visiting my son.

He and his wife have two children. My wife and I are typical grandparents who dote on their grandchildren. But after that last visit, we thought we had been on a tour of duty in Rwanda. They had no manners—and little respect for elders. They communicated by screaming. They were constantly grabbing what the other one had. I couldn't understand why their parents didn't reprimand them, but the parents seemed to have solved the problem just by tuning them out.

Sadly, I had to admit that my grandchildren were little assholes. I am afraid this is true pretty much across the board. It is a lost generation.

In all too many cases, the kids of today have closed their minds to learning new ideas. They are rude and punctuate their rudeness with violence. They are self-absorbed bullies who believe that the world owes them everything.

Believe me, I wish this weren't true. I hate to think that we have lost a whole generation to assholism.

How did it happen?

The assholes got together—and stuck.

Secretly, without the rest of us knowing it, they have formed an organization to promote divisiveness and unrest in society—and to spread assholism into every major institution in humanity.

- They have taken over religion. They are strangling the Catholic Church with the issues of birth control and abortion, they have perverted the message of love into one of hate and bigotry in the fundamentalist sects, and they have spread misinformation and distortion about the nature of God through all denominations.
- They have taken over education. The curriculum has been gutted, the freedom to think has been mugged, and teenagers in school fear for their lives.
- They have taken over politics. It doesn't matter to the assholes which party is in power, just so long as it continues to tyrannize the people by a) raising taxes, b) abridging Constitutional rights, and c) promoting divisiveness among the people.
- They have taken over the arts. There are still individual artists, musicians, and writers who are pursuing their creative muse, but the funding and support of this work has largely fallen into the hands of assholes.
- They have taken over industry, at both the worker and the management level. How else can the demise of Eastern Airlines be explained? The drop in the value of the dollar?
- They have taken over psychology. They have convinced us that anger is healthy, that immaturity is a plausible alternative to adulthood, and that one way or another, we are all victims.
- Above all, they have taken over the media. Both TV and the print media have stooped to running speculation, gossip, and opinion, rather than hard news.

I have come to this conclusion most reluctantly.

Being a decent human being, I want to believe that society is noble and good, and rewards its members who make worthwhile contributions. After all, I am a doctor—a proctologist first and then a psychiatrist—and a doctor must believe in the potential of his patients to get well.

I want to believe that assholism appears only randomly in society—that there is no grand design to subvert life as we know it. I want to believe it, but I cannot. I know better. There is a conspiracy of assholes at work in the world, and it is real.

The more I reflected on this insight, the more I have come to understand it. In fact, it has become so clear to me that I wonder why I am the first person to figure it out. How could the rapid decline on all fronts of society occur otherwise? After all, decent human beings have always outnumbered the assholes—even now, when assholism is on such a rapid rise.

This interpretation of my dream was confirmed in a very unusual way. I was working late one afternoon, as I was scheduled to fly out the next day to deliver an address to the New York State Psychiatric Association on recent advances in treating assholism. I was putting the finishing touches on my speech when my secretary buzzed me. She said there was a man in the outer office who was insisting on seeing me.

"I don't have the time," I said. "Make an appointment for him."

"He insists he cannot wait. He seems desperate to see you, sir."

And desperate he was. He had the demeanor of a hunted man, a man who keeps looking over his shoulder to see who is gaining on him. I assured him he was safe in my office and offered him a drink to calm his nerves. He refused it.

Joe—obviously not his real name—was on the faculty of a local university, where he taught political science. He had graduated near the top of his class at Harvard, and was a rising star as a young professor, too. He had published several articles in major journals and had written a controversial book on the heroes of multi-culturalism. He had been unafraid to stand up for his beliefs and thoughts, even when they were unpopular and heavily criticized by the press.

But none of this achievement was visible as he sat before me, sharing his story. He was nervous, uncertain—scared. Something had clearly happened to shake him to his marrow.

"It was just after I had confirmed my interest in tenure," Joe began. "One of the senior professors in the department called me into his office for some 'friendly advice'—advice that would help me in my effort to acquire tenure.

" 'Ever since Machiavelli,' the professor began, 'political science has been viewed as the exercise of power to change society. We expect you to demonstrate this basic maxim to your students.'

" 'Demonstrate it?'

" 'Yes. We have noted a tendency on your part to challenge your students to think—to understand the issues.'

" 'I try my best.'

" 'Well, stop it!' the professor scolded. 'We don't want our students *thinking,* for God's sake. It's our role to shape and manipulate their *beliefs* —not to encourage them to think on their own.'

14

"He then proceeded to outline a broad scheme of propaganda in which I was to promote divisiveness, support rebelliousness, induce contempt for tradition, reject basic human values, and promote despair in my classes, articles, and lectures. In addition, he told me that I was to identify the most promising malcontents in my classes and direct them to him."

"How did you respond to this strange request?"

"I frankly couldn't believe my ears," Joe responded. "I could not understand why this chap was so interested in controling the minds and beliefs of his students. Was it a weird idiosyncrasy? Or was it something less benign?

"I put the issue to the test by reporting back to the professor on several occasions, each time taping our discussion on a microcassette recorder. He was a sly character all right—he managed to slither by most questions without revealing much. But eventually he let it slip out—and I was able to hear the confirmation of my suspicions with my own ears:

" 'The Association is very grateful for the leads you've provided. Keep up the good work, my boy— and it won't just be tenure in your stocking at Christmas. The Association has more power and wealth than you would believe. If you continue to help out, you will get your just share.'

" 'Just what is the Association?' I asked.

" 'As far as you are concerned,' the professor said, 'I am. There are others, of course, but you don't need to know who they are. Just do what we ask, and we will be pleased. You will be pleased, too.'

"It was at that moment that I realized I was being sucked into a mafia of assholes. I left as quickly as I could without being obvious and drove down here to see you. I had heard you talk about assholism a year ago. I figured that if anyone knew anything about this Association, it must be you. I just hope you aren't part of it, too."

I assured Joe that I was not, and I thanked him for taking me into his confidence.

"You have helped me expose one of the greatest secret conspiracies of all time," I said.

"So it is real after all?" Joe gasped.

"It is indeed. The assholes are not just trying to take over the political science department at your college; they have invaded every single human institution. They are already controling and directing major segments of human life and thought."

"Is there time to stop them?" Joe implored.

"I pray that there is," I answered. "And you'd better pray, too."

Part One:
How Assholes
Infect Society

1
The Root of All Evil

How many feminists does it take to screw in a light bulb?
Seven. One to do the work, one to give her comfort, and five to issue a press release blaming men for inventing and manufacturing light bulbs that need changing.

Society struggles to cope with many serious problems, from hunger and illiteracy to overpopulation and war. As we have tried to understand these problems and produce solutions, we have speculated on many possible root causes for them:

Poverty.

Ignorance.

Racism.

Sexism.

Class struggle.

The devil.

Whole philosophies, such as Marxism, have evolved to propose strategies for eliminating these causes. But they have all failed and collapsed, for

18

a very good reason. None of these six causes is the actual root of evil in humanity.

The real cause of humanity's woes and suffering is plain and simple.

There are too many assholes.

As long as they operate on a free-lance basis, pursuing their own selfish goals, they do not pose much of a threat. They create a lot of mischief and pain, of course, but nothing that a nation or a race can't survive.

The real danger arises when assholes begin to clump together. Then they become a frightening power—one that should alarm every intelligent decent human being. Assholes are past masters at stirring up trouble in otherwise peaceful situations, to the point where decent people begin to question and accuse one another and point fingers. Once the assholes succeed in stirring up mischief, they fade into the background and let the decent human beings carry the battle from both sides.

This is certainly true in the abortion issue, where we have witnessed the spectacle of "pro-lifers" assaulting and even killing medical professionals who offer to perform abortions. Both the pro-life and the pro-abortion factions have valid arguments for their positions. What both sides lack is a stronger respect for their fellow human beings. This lack of respect, then, has been seized and carefully orchestrated by the assholes among us, so that each side appears to the other side to be demons. The assholes have used their rhetoric to convince both sides that there is no common ground on which this issue could be resolved. It therefore remains an unhealed schism tearing apart our society.

This is how we talk about the abortion controversy, and how the press reports it. But it is not really a social controversy; it is mainly an *asshole controversy*—an issue that has been inflamed and kept alive by assholes.

If you examine most of the major issues that divide us today, sooner or later you will reach the same conclusion:

The hidden cause behind these problems is always assholism, the root of all evil.

It is sometimes hard to see this truth at first, because assholes are so sly and clever in hiding their tracks. They operate by hit-and-run, causing major damage to the commonweal without leaving any marks that incriminate them.

The perfect example of this is the mischief they have caused in our national sense of humor. It used to be that we could laugh about our differences, whether they be sexual, racial, ethnic, or religious. But somewhere in the last twenty years, society has reversed its opinion. If we tell a joke that *anyone* takes offense to, we are now guilty of abusing that poor individual. If this should happen:

- We can be fired from our job.
- We can be forced to resign from our government post.
- We can be kicked out of college.

Even though we live in a democracy, I do not recall voting on this change in social attitude over the last two decades. Can you?

Can you even remember Congress voting on it? Did we all sleep through the Ban All Humor (BAH) bill of 1983?

No. It was the work of assholes.

It was likewise the assholes who managed to convince large segments of society that it is okay to:

- Make fun of men, but not women.
- Make fun of whites, but not blacks, Hispanics, Indians, Asian-Americans, and Creoles.
- Make fun of Christians, but never Jews, Moslems, or atheists—but especially Jews. If you do that, then you are automatically an anti-Semite.
- Make fun of big business, but never the working people.
- Make fun of conservatives, but not liberals.

Assholes have always existed, of course, but they have seldom been as well organized as they are today. It is the unseen emergence of the Association that brings cause for alarm. Somewhere, probably in the mountains of West Virginia (but certainly not very far from Washington, the world epicenter of assholism), there are actually asshole compounds where they train mere bullies to become asshole agents. Over the past two decades, these asshole agents have begun to infiltrate every institution and power center of our society.

These assholes work quietly, behind the scenes. They could be living right next to you, without you even knowing—perhaps even in your own household! But they are quietly pressing their own secret agenda, without us even suspecting it.

If we do not recognize this threat now, and do something about it, we will wake up one fine morning in the not too distant future, and discover a sad fact:

We have become a nation of assholes!

2
The Asshole's Accomplice

> If a blonde dyes her hair, how can you tell that she is still a dumb blonde?
> She believes what she reads in the papers.

On their own, assholes could not have possibly achieved this level of influence in society. Individually, assholes are so selfish, mule-headed, and obnoxious that they find it very difficult to work together. Asking an asshole to cooperate, even with other assholes, is like asking IRS agents to be fair. It's against their nature.

Unfortunately, the disruptive activities of the assholes have been made easier by an all too willing accomplice: the mass media. The newspapers, magazines, and broadcast stations of this country are like a free platform for assholes, available to them whenever they wish to use it.

Decent human beings do not generally have this kind of access to the press. They almost have to be killed before the media will pay attention to them and the work they are doing. Assholes, on the other hand, are universally regarded as good copy.

In part, this is because there is a very high percentage of assholes in the media. You have to be a fairly accomplished bully asshole to survive in that environment, after all—to be able to push and shove your way through a large crowd of other assholes—namely, your journalistic peers.

A good television journalist will have no qualms at all about coaching the participants at a protest rally how to shout and scream most dramatically before the cameras. So it did not take long for the assholes to realize that they could always count on the press to a) cover their point of view on any story and b) distort their message into something even more outrageous than it was to begin with.

Nowhere was this more evident than in the way that the media covered the story of the homeless in my hometown. Now, I have been to San Francisco and New York and seen the bums and bag ladies sleeping on the streets. But I have never seen this type of poor unfortunate in my own city.

Nevertheless, when the cause of the homeless became a national issue a few years ago, our local daily assigned a reporter to investigate the homeless problem in our town.

The reporter called the Y, the Salvation Army, and other agencies that have traditionally dealt with this problem in the past. No one seemed aware of any significant problem of permanent homelessness, not just in our city but in the whole region.

Nonetheless, word quickly circulated that the reporter was investigating homelessness. Within only a few hours, it had reached the ears of one of our local asshole agitators. Sensing the opportunity at hand, he hastily called a news conference for the following morning.

At the press conference, the asshole announced that he had been troubled by the problem of homelessness in our city for years. He criticized the local elected officials harshly for letting such a problem fester without taking action. He cited statistics of homelessness which were clearly figments of his imagination, referring to the thousands of people who are trapped by "this pitiful inhumanity." Then he announced that he was forming a committee to fight the problem and would be accepting donations to help the needy. He set a goal at $500,000 a year.

During the question and answer part of the news conference, a reporter from a local TV station did inquire into the source of his statistics. Without blinking an eye, the asshole listed a number of plausible sources, none of which either existed or had ever published the reports he cited. But his citations sounded impressive, and they were reported as fact both in the newspaper and by the television station.

Money started pouring in to fight homelessness. The asshole, of course, never spent the first dime on the homeless—they didn't exist, after all. Most of the money was actually spent on remodeling his own home. When questioned, years later, about the seeming impropriety of his use of the money, he answered simply that most of the funding went to "administrative costs."

But the real cost was not to be found in money extorted from decent but gullible human beings. It came in the form of controversy and divisiveness. As money poured into his front organization, the legitimate social agencies that had successfully managed the problem in the first place began to be ignored. They started having budget problems, and programs had to be cut. Soon, there were the beginnings of a genuine homeless problem.

The elected officials who were held up for ridicule at the press conference were, of course, thrown out of office at the next election. They were replaced by assholes who stirred up even greater mischief.

Predictably, the churches rushed to jump on the bandwagon, not wanting to appear uncharitable toward the homeless. When several members of one church openly questioned the possibility that the church had been duped, they were thrown out of the congregation and became the subject of the pastor's hellfire and brimstone for weeks and weeks.

The folks in my hometown still do not know the true facts about the homeless—or hunger in America, for that matter. They live in an information bubble that was blown up by an asshole and kept inflated by the media. The dilemma of the homeless and the hungry is now being taught in our elementary and high schools as though it were fact— and something important to know.

Never underestimate the power of the press in helping assholes subvert and control your thinking.

3
What Assholes Want

How do you know when assholes are
being considerate?
They tap you on the shoulder before
shoving you out of the way.
—*Dr. Crement's Pocket Guide To
Surviving Assholes*

The most common question I am asked as I tour
the country lecturing and holding ANAL workshops
is:

What do assholes really want?

What do they hope to gain by stirring up mischief
and inciting unrest throughout society?

This is a good question, but one that is based on
the values and thinking of decent people. Assholes
are different. They do not want anything in specific.
They want everything.

Rational people, of course, understand that no
person needs everything, just a reasonable share of
it. "Reasonable share" is a concept that does not
exist in the minds or hearts of assholes. It is beyond
their grasp.

In fact, lots of things that ordinary humans

accept as natural are missing and unaccounted for in assholes. Two of the most important are:

1. Humane values.
2. Intelligence.

Although assholes can be clever in a manipulative, you-can't-pin-the-blame-on-me kind of way, they don't actually think. They never wonder about what they are doing or why they are doing it. As a result, they do not know where they are going or what they want, except in the most superficial, self-absorbed way.

When pressed for an answer, of course, an asshole will never admit that he has no goals or values. So he or she will aspire to something that sounds like a goal or principle, but just reflects self-absorption:

Money.

Sex.

Power.

Or, if they are really greedy, they will mention all three, adding, "What else is there?"

The key to understanding assholes is to realize that to an asshole, there is nothing else. Values such as loyalty, goodwill, or wisdom mean nothing. The goal of making a lasting, enlightened contribution at work or in the community—even just by raising a good family—is incomprehensible to assholes. They understand only three little words:

Take, take, take!

When they talk about money, what they mean is: "I will take your money now."

When they talk about sex, what they mean is: "I want to take you *now*."

When they talk about power, what they mean is: "If you have any, I'm going to take it."

Never let yourself be caught in a give-and-take situation with an asshole—as in a marriage or a work partnership. Assholes will interpret it in only one way: you give and they take.

Herein lies the whole dirty secret of assholism: they operate on the three keynotes of ignorance, laziness, and greed. They are too ignorant to know what they want, though, so they decide to want what everyone else wants—namely, what decent people want.

Being ignorant, they perceive only the results of honest labor and efforts: material rewards, friendships, and authority.

Being greedy, they want these rewards—of money, sex, and power—immediately and in large amounts.

Here is the kicker, though—they are too lazy to earn any of these things. Even worse, because they are ignorant, they assume there must be a trick to getting what they want. They want a *deal!* They want the thrill of cheating others out of whatever it is they want. So they adopt an adversarial, competitive style, provoking decent people into playing *their* game, thereby validating their chosen ethics and lifestyle. This is what the asshole calls a "win/win situation."

Some assholes will accept a consolation, however. Finding that they cannot actually take away money, sex, or power from you, they will content themselves simply with spoiling your enjoyment of it.

It is important to understand the innate envy and competitiveness of the individual asshole in order to grasp the enormity of the threat of the

28

asshole conspiracy. There is no benevolence or purpose in the actions of the Association. Their objective is a simple one: to steal and destroy as much of what we decent people value and hold dear as they can.

In America, this generally means undermining the very principles and values on which this country was founded. The conspiracy of assholes is working steadily to distort the significance of *justice,* so that it ends up meaning "special privileges," not fairness. They are blurring the meaning of *responsibility,* so that productive people become obliged to support lazy people. They are undermining the concept of *charity,* so that it means endless indulgence of every parasite. They are sabotaging the significance of *tolerance,* so that we end up permitting every intolerant malcontent to dictate correct behavior and policy to the rest of us.

Slowly, we are being conned into giving up our freedoms in order to "protect the victims" of all manner of exaggerated and wholly imaginary offenses. Once these freedoms are gone, it will be unlikely that we can recover them.

I fear that they have succeeded far more than we dare imagine.

4
Spotting Assholes

> How can you tell you've been talking
> with assholes?
> From the teethmarks they leave all
> over your body.
> —*Dr. Crement's Pocket Guide To
> Surviving Assholes*

The second most frequently asked question at my lectures and workshops is:

"It is easy enough to spot a rude, obnoxious, troublemaking asshole. But some assholes do not stand out so blatantly. How can you tell they are assholes before you have exposed yourself to real damage?"

There is no simple answer. I myself have been duped by asshole colleagues who took my ANAL classes on the completely believable pretext that they wanted to give up their assholism. But that was not their motive at all. They just wanted to steal my ideas and methodologies.

Three months after taking my class, they were offering their own seminars. The only problem was that no one ever seemed to recover. They had so misunderstood my ideas, especially the ones about goodwill and decency, that they were just reinforcing the asshole behavior of their students—and teaching them how to pass themselves off as decent human beings.

It is important to understand that not all assholes are flaming and obnoxious. As I explained in my first book, *Asshole No More*, there are situational assholes—people who only exhibit asshole traits in specific sets of circumstances—and there are sissy assholes—people who manipulate you by overplaying the victim role. I have had to help many a person try to put their lives back together again after they had been all but destroyed by a sissy asshole.

So I warn people that assholes come in all colors and styles, in all degrees of intensity. It is a mistake to think that all assholes resemble mad dogs, openly displaying their lust for power through intimidation and bullying. These obnoxious people are easy to spot, as they try to clobber us with their private impersonation of Attila the Hun—or even worse, pursue their idea of social responsibility to save some endangered species of worm. If we fail to stay away from them, we have no one to blame but ourselves.

But who can be blamed for being sucked in and deceived by a sissy asshole—an asshole who manages to make a career of dependency out of an easily curable problem? Sissy assholes are the kind of people who require weeks of bed care and attention just to recover from a hangnail. Their concept of "sharing" is to find a way to trap you into giving them all of your attention and energy—while they are exempted from most adult responsibilities.

31

It is likewise very hard to detect situational assholes until it is too late. This is because these assholes behave like decent human beings most of the time—right up to the moment when something goes wrong. Then the full impact of their assholism will be felt, as they deny any responsibility for the problem and make sure that you receive every bit of the blame for screwing up.

Naturally, these patterns carry over into the ways assholism has corrupted society. The carefully orchestrated "rights" of the welfare generation are a perfect example of sissy assholism at work on a grand scale—right down to the fact that society has now embraced the idea of unilateral sharing. Somehow, it has become a "right" of the welfare generation to "share" in the money the rest of us make by working, without simultaneously sharing in the work!

As for situational assholism, it has never been more masterfully exercised than by the women's movement. When Joan Dailey died during a liposuction operation a year ago, how long did it take Gloria Stoneham to denounce it as the "inevitable tragedy of living in a male dominated society"? Less than an hour. And she never explained how she could make such a declaration when the doctor was a woman. But she didn't have to. She is an asshole.

A full list of the characteristics of the asshole is printed in *Asshole No More*. But in the years since that book was published, I have developed a shorter list—of five sure signs of assholism. These five signs will enable you to spot the asshole within a person even when it is cleverly disguised.

They will also help you begin to see the evidence

that assholism is strangling our social well-being.

The five are:

1. Jealousy. The one thing assholes cannot abide is the success of someone else. Asshole parents will ridicule the achievements of their children; asshole colleagues will find something in your accomplishments to complain about. If nothing else, they will chide you for your lack of humility—or imply that you came by your success unfairly, stealing it from someone more deserving. The tell-tale sign that you have been exposed to a jealous asshole is to check your guilt meter after being around one for awhile. If it is overheating, you can be sure he or she is an asshole.

In society, the constant effort to tarnish the image of entrepreneurs, creative people, and high achievers, so that the unproductive won't feel bad, is a chilling example of this tell-tale sign.

2. Competitiveness. Whatever it is that they want, assholes believe there is only a finite amount to be acquired. As a result, they want to be the first, and if possible, the only one to attain it. They long to be "king of the mountain," even if it means shoving everyone else into a ditch to get there. In point of fact, they enjoy shoving others aside. To them, cheating is winning—and winning is everything. The competitive assholes are adroit at taking credit for work they did not do—and shifting blame to others for mistakes they made all on their own. They thrive on crisis, making sure they cut a highly visible profile, but if the crisis takes a turn for the worse, they are prepared with elaborate excuses to duck the blame. As valuable as they try to make themselves appear, most of their success has noth-

33

ing to do with any effort they have made. In other words, the success would have occurred even if they had been at home, sick. They are past masters of the art of hype, creating wonderful illusions out of a brown cloud of bullshit.

The tell-tale sign that you are being crapped on by competitive assholes is the level of indignation with which they respond when you point out their deficiencies. Competitive assholes, being creatures of hype, cannot stand criticism of any kind. If you criticize their lack of results, you will be accused of being insensitive to the enormous burden they shoulder. If you criticize their lack of competence, you will be condemned for being arrogant and judgmental. If you expose their excuses, you will be attacked as rude and prejudiced. And if you should catch them stealing ideas or taking credit for work they did not do, you will be lambasted for your disloyalty as a friend or, even worse, co-conspirator. As Adolph Schneider so artfully puts it in his book, *Assholes I Have Known,* competitive assholes set it up so that they always win and you always lose.

On the larger scale, the tell-tale sign of competitive assholism can be seen among many of the leaders of the feminist movement, who try to establish equality through male bashing, demands for special treatment, and a deluge of misinformation about the status of women in society.

3. Exploitation. Assholes love to exploit problems. It could be the problems of others, where the asshole lends money at usurious rates, or it could be their own problem, making a career out of a misfortune or disability. Just look at the number of people who have become specialists in counseling people

34

who suffer from grief. Most of them do not know the first thing about grief, except that those suffering from it will pay lots of money in the hope of being relieved of it. That's exploitation.

The tell-tale sign of the exploitative asshole is that they have no authentic help to offer. If people get over their grief, it is only because they have healed themselves; the majority of clients the asshole therapist sees register no improvement. It must always be remembered that good, decent therapists—grief or otherwise—actually offer their clients concrete help. Their goal is to assist the client to get well. The goal of the asshole is to hang onto a paying customer as long as possible.

In society, these assholes exploit whole groups and movements. They operate like the city councilman in my hometown, who chaired the airport commission. During his years on council, the airport tripled in size and quadrupled in activity. Coincidentally, several phantom companies that he created provided the airport with millions of dollars in services during that time.

4. Dishonesty. Assholes are inherently dishonest. They lack the inner morality that would prevent them from cheating. In fact, if they stumble across a potential opportunity, they consider it their *duty* to seize and exploit it, no matter how many laws or rules they must break.

It must be understood that dishonesty is an innate trait of assholes. Even if you ask them a simple question about the weather, assholes will deliberately lie—just so they know something you do not. In this same vein, they will often withhold information you need—like failing to pass on tele-

35

phone messages. This gives them more opportunities to blame you for dropping the ball when you fail to return an important call.

On a larger scale, the Internal Revenue Service likewise embodies dishonest assholism. Chartered by law to collect taxes, the IRS operates on the belief that they are above the law. And so, they routinely break at least half of the liberties guaranteed us by the Bill of Rights. This breach is not just the over-zealousness of a few fanatic agents; it is written into the policies and procedures of the agency itself. Apparently, the motto of the IRS is: "If you cheat, you pay. If we cheat, you still pay." It is a perfect asshole creed.

The tell-tale sign of asshole dishonesty is the use of double and triple standards. If you make a mistake on your tax return, you may face criminal charges—even prison time, as Leona Helmesley found out. But when massive malfeasance and abuse is discovered in the ranks of the IRS, as it recently was in the Southeast section, a few employees are retired early and the rest are given promotions! Honest people would accept such mistakes openly—and even try to make amends. Assholes just cover up.

5. Bullshit. Assholes love to bullshit—in fact, according to H.M. Rhoid, author of *Assholes Among Us,* it may be the only real talent assholes have. They know when to wax indignant and when to whine and act hurt. They can invent sympathy and flattery on the spot, and never hesitate to use fear, doubt, anger, and guilt whenever they will prove valuable.

At the group level, bullshit is relabeled "propaganda," but it all smells the same. Most of what we read in newspapers and magazines is propaganda, not facts. Most of what politicians tell us is bullshit, not facts. But propaganda doesn't have to stick to the facts, for it is not its purpose to inform or clarify. Its purpose is to persuade.

Whenever an asshole speaks, you can be sure he or she is bullshitting. But how can we spot the bullshit artist in the first place? Many of these propaganda assholes have refined persuasion to a subtle art. The tell-tale sign is that they are trying to make an unnatural impact on us. Everything they say is an effort to manipulate us—to play upon our fears, desires, guilt, or anger. If, after we have been talking with someone, we feel as though they have just recruited us to their cause—even though we do not know just what it is—we have been conned by an asshole.

In a perfect society, assholes would be required to wear a scarlet letter "A," so that decent human beings could detect them without trouble. Even then, of course, the assholes would undoubtedly try to bullshit their way out of this limitation, by trying to make us believe that only "chosen people" can wear the letter, or some such hogwash. But we live in an asshole society, so we must take care. Assholes can only succeed as assholes if there are decent human beings who are willing to be conned.

As Sidney Koan puts it in his book, *Zen and the Art of Being an Asshole,* "Knowledge is the key to everything. Until you can recognize shit on a stick, you are likely to get hit with both."

5
Mr. Tom

Beware of assholes with a cause.
—*The Joy of Protest,* by Henry
Buttercup

Once I had met Joe, I stopped having nightmares about jackasses. The dreams, however, were replaced by a chilly sensation that enveloped me whenever I was alone. I am not one to cave into paranoia readily, but I felt as if I were being watched by invisible eyes. Every time I tried to focus on the eyes that were not there, I thought they were somehow linked with the Association, whatever it was. But I knew this couldn't be true, so I dismissed these thoughts and plunged myself back into my regular work routine.

Only a few weeks had passed when my awareness of the Association was suddenly broadened. Harrison Honda, a friend of mine, asked me to accompany him to a special directors' meeting at the local Salvation Army. He was a member of the board.

As we drove to the meeting, he explained that he

had been approached by a prominent black leader—leader of color, I should say—who had asked him to set up the meeting. Smelling something foul, Harry wanted my support and insight.

I will not name this man, for he is well-known. His trademark is the phrase, "victims of society's neglect," which he uses often in his speeches and interviews.

I will just call him Tom.

I had heard rumors about Mr. Tom—the Rolls Royces, the diamonds, the mistresses, and the drugs. But I couldn't imagine why he would be coming to a Salvation Army meeting. Surely he wasn't about to reform!

I was correct. Mr. Tom arrived with a flourish and four bodyguards, whom he introduced as his "associates." My ears pricked up immediately, but I disregarded the connection I had made. I wanted to be fair, unbiased.

The alarm sounded again when Mr. Tom, looking quite prosperous in his $1200 suit and silk shirt, asked that the meeting be off the record—that no notes should be taken of what was said. My interest had been grabbed, to say the least.

Mr. Tom spoke first of the "great need" of the vast hordes of disadvantaged people in the city—and the desperate need for charitable organizations to help more than they have in the past. Everyone in the room concurred, although no one seemed to regard it as a startling observation.

But then Mr. Tom put on the squeeze play. "Blacks and Hispanics resent having to grovel before rich white folks, because they know, rightly or wrongly, that they are the same folks who held them back, exploited their labor, and neglected their needs for so long." He paused. "And women resent having to go to men for assistance for the same reason.

"We feel that a lot more would be accomplished if blacks could come to blacks for help, and women could come to women." (He missed a beat when he forgot to remention the Hispanics.)

Mr. Tom then proceeded to propose that day-to-day management of the local Salvation Army be turned over to his organization. This, he claimed, would result in "better public relations and more goodwill" among the community—by which he meant his people.

Naturally, the board would continue—it was needed to raise money. But the funds raised would be turned over to Mr. Tom.

I could tell that the board members were flabbergasted by the blatant, asshole attempt to take over their agency, but they covered it well. One of them made a few polite comments, and then moved to table the proposal.

Mr. Tom seemed ready. "I do not think you understand my offer. We are in a position to maintain peace and harmony in the community—if you cooperate with us. If you do not, then we cannot be responsible for what might happen as the discontent and militancy of these poor, exploited people grows.

"I'm not saying there would be riots or boycotts, but my people are restless. They are ready to fight for their rights. And I, for one, am ready to help them.

"Do you understand me better now?"

I sure as hell did, and so did everyone else at the table. But Harry was determined not to be pushed around. He asked if all comments were truly off the record. Smiling, Mr. Tom agreed. Then Harry made his reply, very quietly:

"We can recognize threats when we hear them, and have no intention of caving into yours. We are willing to meet with anyone who wishes to discuss the true grievances of the poor. But if you are an agent of anyone other than your own self-interest, I'll be damned."

"You said it," Mr. Tom smiled. "Not I. I can assure you that I have far greater power than you can imagine—power far greater than the poor and disadvantaged could give me. After all, they are poor and disadvantaged. What power do they have?

"I am part of an Association that controls the media, the politicians, social activists, and even the churches. The turmoil that followed the Rodney King verdict in Los Angeles is an example of the power of this organization. I suggest you take my proposal more seriously."

And with that he left, sweeping out with his retinue.

Harry turned to me. "X," he said, "What do you think of our Mr. Tom? Is he a nut case? Or is he serious? Does he really have the power to take on the Salvation Army—and win?"

I took a deep breath.

"I've heard of this Association that he mentioned, and from what I can tell, it is a collection of assholes that are just as psychopathic as he is. Nationwide, they seem to have a lot of influence in very high places. Mr. Tom may well be exaggerating

41

his strength, but I for one would not count on it. If you decide not to cooperate with him, I suggest you make sure your insurance is up to date—and has a big pay off.

"You can rely on one thing. Trouble is brewing, and it's all thanks to assholes."

Part Two:
A New Theory
Of Social Evolution

6
Asshole Bonding

> Once you step into the asshole's
> arena—of fear, guilt, or anger—then
> he is able to play by his rules—and
> cheat you.
> —*Buddy, Can You Spare a Para-
> digm?* by Charles Dyslexus

I have spent my whole life surrounded by assholes. In fact, I was one myself before I reformed. I
know assholes better than anyone else. I therefore
have no problem accepting the idea of an Association of assholes—except one.

How do they get together? How to they stick
together so that they can actually operate effec-
tively as an organization?

You have to keep in mind that if two assholes
marry each other, they will either be dead, divorced,
or crazy within two years.

If two assholes go into business together, they
will end up destroying the company by suing each
other—or committing suicide.

There is no such thing as genuine friendship

among assholes; at best, it is a shared spirit of competitiveness and greed. But they will always be jealous and suspicious of each other. They can't help it—unless they go into recovery.

So how does this Association manage to stay together? How do these assholes repress the most powerful elements in their character, and actually get along with one another? After all, to the average asshole, "cooperate" means "you do what I tell you."

I believe the answer is evolutionary—that a small but growing number of visionary assholes have evolved over the centuries. These visionary assholes, or Super Browns, as I like to call them, are able to see past their petty predatory instincts and appreciate the possibilities of universal preying. Having affixed their lust and greed on total social domination, it is a small, unimportant matter for them to learn the necessary sacrifices this will require:

• Learning to accept other assholes as friends and colleagues.

• Faking the virtuous qualities of decent human beings.

• Acquiring the patience required to control major sociological movements. It took a long time to stock the court system with assholes, for instance, but that was the only effective way the Association could actually corrupt our legal system.

Once I saw it in this light, my doubts began to evaporate. After all, ordinary thieves are able to band together—so why not assholes? Even in the Stone Age, gangs of thugs probably organized themselves to raid other camps and families—just as they still do in Los Angeles and other major cities.

45

Actually, the evidence that assholes do bond with one another is fairly staggering. When commercial traffic developed on the high seas, assholes invented piracy to prey on the ships. It is hard to imagine forty assholes crammed in one small frigate, but apparently they learned to get along.

Indeed, as society advanced, both the thieves and the assholes (often one and the same) refined their organizations and developed larger and more powerful syndicates:

- The mafia.
- The unions.
- The Church.

And, as power became more concentrated in government and religion, assholes leaped in to "help govern the masses and redeem the sinners." How else can we explain such absurdities as religious wars—the Crusades in Christianity, the jihads in Islam—and the oppression of heretics?

The assholes did it.

Little by little, I believe, assholes have maneuvered themselves into positions of power in all major branches of society. In the past, this was limited primarily to government and religion, but in recent times, it has spread into business, education, and most recently, the arts and the media.

This is not all. Recent events, some of which I have already described, have led me to believe that this is not a fluke of evolution. It is a conspiracy that is being perpetrated by a secret lodge or brotherhood of assholes, the Association. The Super Browns.

The actual members of the Association never expose themselves in public. Instead, they prefer to act behind the scenes, working through willing

46

agents. They grow by recruiting and training assholes on the make, and then help them rise to prominence and influence in their respective fields. These protégés in turn recruit, promote, and protect younger assholes as they find them. The evidence available to me suggests that they seize almost every opportunity that arises to promote and protect their own kind.

This secret society is the Association. It is international in scope, and in fact has gained a very large foothold in the United Nations. They play the game internationally, no longer thinking of themselves as French assholes or German assholes or American assholes. Assholism is their country, their faith, and their passion. They are married to it.

What hard evidence do we have of the operations of the Association? Almost none. But who else than a bunch of assholes could be behind such absurd and destructive therapies as primal scream? In this therapy, you are taught to flip around on the floor like a grounded dolphin, recreating the birth struggle. In this way, you are supposed to get in touch with your screaming inner infant. As you cry and scream, this is supposed to somehow release your pent-up happiness and maturity, leading to a cure.

Who else than a bunch of assholes could be responsible for the disappearance of thinking from our college campuses, where relativism has become the norm for judging all ideas and events? According to this "new thought," nothing has any meaning until each one of us invents it; there is no truth except what you want to believe. And the truth can vary for each us. If my truth offends you, then it is my duty to revise what I believe so that you are no longer offended. It is a perfect asshole trap—and one that wipes out 2,500 years of Platonic thought and progress in human understanding.

Who else than a bunch of assholes could convince hard-nosed business people that you actually can win through intimidation? Those who tried discovered the painful fact that the targets of their intimidation often had the ways and means to fight back—and win. For this reason, we no longer hear the phrase "winning through intimidation," but it is still alive and well. It has just been given new labels.

Who else than a bunch of assholes could successfully advocate such flagrantly misanthropic ideas as: "All men are vicious beasts whose primary satisfaction comes from exploiting women?"

Who else but a bunch of assholes could keep alive the flames of conflicts hundreds of years old, and reignite them into warfare and civil strife, not just in one or two places but in countries throughout the world?

Who but a bunch of assholes would have the nerve to claim that women could never be sexists or that blacks could never be racists?

The answer is simple. No one. Only well-trained and heavily supported assholes, working together in some sort of confederation, could cause such mischief.

As a former proctologist, I know all too well that you don't actually have to stick your finger up someone's ass to know what it is. It is true that the Association does not advertise. But we do not need such blatant proof to know that it exists.

They have managed to get their message across.

7
Playing Both Ends

> In the Sixties, we thought only good things—and great changes—were "blowin' in the breeze." Now, it turns out, we were just downwind from a bunch of assholes.
> —John Fluck, in *It Ain't the Sixties Anymore, Susie*

They say you need to think like a fish in order to be a good fisherman. I know a few experienced fly fishermen who seem to have achieved that uncanny ability.

The same is true of assholes. To fully understand them and their conspiracy, you have to think like one. Not like the ordinary asshole, who is too preoccupied with money, sex, and power to take the time to think, but the Super Browns, who had the vision to plot the domination of the whole world.

Being a reformed asshole, I still have—if I strain—the ability to think in asshole ways. I always pay dearly when I use it—I have a crushing headache for three days or more. But on occasion, it has given me worthwhile insights.

It certainly did in this case.

One night, as I was pondering the nature of the Association, I nodded off at my desk. While asleep, I dreamed I was watching a group of apes. They would catch birds by putting out grain for them; then, while the birds were snacking, the apes would capture them and strip off all their wing feathers. Unable to fly, the birds would then wander around helplessly, in great distress, until the apes killed and ate them.

When I looked more closely, I saw that the bits of grain had words on them. I asked one of the apes what the words meant. "Nothing," he replied. "They are just the lure—these birds believe they can eat their way to knowledge. Pretty stupid, huh? But once we control both wings, we also control the body. It's just that simple."

He turned away and went back to pulling wing feathers off more birds. Feathers floated every-where, and as I looked beyond him, I saw a huge pile of bird skeletons. Shuddering at the bleak sight, I snapped out of my dream.

I sat up and involuntarily cried out, "Eureka," even though I was nowhere close to a bathtub. I had acquired the "missing link" in my conspiracy theory.

On their own, assholes must try to trick each decent human being one on one. They may succeed for a while, but eventually the target tires of being conned and fights back. The assholes are apt to lose as often as they win—perhaps more often.

When organized, however, assholes can play both ends of every game. They infiltrate both ex-tremes of any issue, institution, or group, and then radicalize it. They engage the assholes at the other extreme with attacks, accusations, and confrontation.

Keep in mind that none of the assholes on either extreme care one whit about the issues at hand—or the differences which split the rest of the group. They merely want to exploit these schisms and magnify them, so that the decent people involved start arguing, too.

And this is what the decent people do, because they *care* about the issues and principles. Of course, they think they are participating in a debate that will lead to a resolution. Nothing could be further from the truth. They are participating in a staged dispute that is meant to become a riot or revolution.

It's a win/win situation for the Association. No matter which extreme wins, another humane issue or cause has been destroyed—or distorted beyond any recognition. And the decent human beings who have played their parts as pawns in this great asshole drama never even suspect that they have been duped.

It's pure brown genius, I have to admit. Unfortunately, once I had seen the pattern, it was all too easy to see how many times it has been employed.

Look at the issue of gay rights. This never was a major problem in society—until radicals on both sides shoved it right in our face. "Live and let live" was the attitude of most people on this topic, so long as it did not intrude on them. How did this comfortable climate change? The Association stirred up both extremes. It incited militant gays to insist that society give them full recognition and rights, including the right to marry and to have partners covered under insurance and entitlement programs.

At the same time, it pushed militant gay bashers and right wing hysterics to condemn homosexuality and work to deny them any rights at all. Having simultaneously activated both extremes, the Association left everyone in the middle confused, feeling that they must side with one extreme or the other. Instead of sitting down and rationally finding a common ground which would lead to a healing of this social problem, we have let the rhetoric, anger, and bigotry escalate, leaving no sensible middle ground.

Score one for the assholes.

The same pattern exists with the problem of street drugs. It goes without saying that the drug lords and pushers are assholes. What could be a better recruitment tool for assholes than the promise of instant bliss and huge profits? But another group of assholes control the other end as well. They pretend to be revolted by drug usage, but somehow always manage to end up blaming society, not the people on drugs! They preach and screech, but their pious pose is usually just a front for attacking society and undermining its capacity to act. By disguising themselves as "wolves in Mother Teresa's clothing," these assholes are able to extort even more money and power for their own devious purposes.

If the pattern is not yet clear, just remember this: the major force working to solve the drug problem is the government—the ultimate refuge of assholes.

Because the anti-drug assholes claim to be doing everything possible to solve the problem, the good people wait for it to occur. But it isn't going to occur, because the assholes have stolen the war on drugs—and have no intention of ever declaring peace.

Score another for the assholes.

Assholes are masters of the art of faking sincerity and compassion. As a result, they often pose as the leaders of all kinds of social movements, not just the anti-drug campaign. Their goal, always, is to take control of legitimate charities, foundations, and social programs. Isn't it curious that the very people who led protest marches in the Sixties are now administrators of huge government and private programs to promote social welfare? Has the protest march been moved off the streets and into the offices of respectability, without us ever knowing about it—or approving of it?

Who was the real winner of the war on poverty? Assholes!

This is also the case in the battle of pornography. I am no prude; I have been known to tell a dirty joke on occasion, and only recently let my subscription to *Playboy* run out. But there is some vicious, brutal, and disgusting stuff disseminated that is clearly pornographic. The sleazebags that make and distribute it are clearly assholes. But so are the people at the opposite end of the issue, the ones who rant and rave about how pornography is ruining the country, oppressing women, and undermining the morality of our youth.

Indeed, the bigotry and rage of the anti-pornographers is hardly a good example for anyone but rattlesnakes and other assholes!

In between, there is plenty of room for an intelligent public debate about rights and responsibilities. But the middle ground remains strangely vacant. The assholes have managed to pluck off our wing feathers once again.

Look around. For as far as you can see, every major divisive issue in this country has been captured by assholes.

It is a disgrace that racism continues to be a problem, but hardly surprising, given the hidden agenda of the Association. Great strides have been made in creating racial balance in this country, but those achievements are jeopardized by assholes on both sides. When vicious black racists are promoted as role models for young blacks, it is a slam dunk that assholes are involved. When quotas are used to give minorities special treatment not available to everyone else, it is clear that the assholes have once more triumphed.

Even our basic approach to life has been corrupted. We can see it on television, where programs like the *McLaughlin Report* encourage shouting and screaming, instead of debate.

We have let the assholes take control of the game. It's in the late innings, and we are way behind. There is still hope, but only if we act.

Don't wait to see if decency is outlawed.

8
Opiate of the Asses

"Moby Dick is no longer to be considered a major work of American fiction, because it glorifies the destruction of an endangered species."
—Arnold Ahab, writing in the *English Literature Reconstructionist*

From the beginning of time, philosophers have tried to understand how growth occurs in the human race. In the middle of the last century, Charles Darwin advanced his theory of evolution, survival of the fittest, based on his observations of mammoth turtles on the Galapagos Islands. This theory has become an accepted standard, but there are other theories as well. Most of them point to some kind of suffering or hardship that so troubles the individual that he or she is forced to revise beliefs, principles, and even behavior.

Freud, for instance, suggested that the alienation of the adult springs from repressed childhood traumas and the frustration of childhood sexual drives.

Karl Marx was convinced that the struggle of

humanity was stimulated primarily by the exploitation of the working classes by the ruling class.

Today, radical feminists claim that the major cause of all problems in the world is too much testosterone—which is in fact the male hormone, not a new topping for pizza.

And, as always, the fundamentalists blame the devil for every evil under the sun.

There is a certain amount of evidence for all of these suggestions. But when they are thoroughly scrutinized, they all take a wrong turn somewhere short of the truth. They have been caught in the net of the Association, which fed them partial truths which they then expanded into all-embracing theories. But the theories uniformly fail to point to the real cause of all misery in humanity:

Assholes.

Our evolution as a race and culture is designed to move forward much more rapidly than it has. Decent human beings have always outnumbered the assholes, and are supposed to keep them in check. And it isn't a difficult assignment. It just takes a conscious effort to express the steadfastness, generosity, charity, goodwill, and honesty that are inherent traits in good people. If we can do this with any semblance of intelligent planning and coordination, the assholes—and the Association—will be devastated.

I am not overlooking the fact that society—especially government, the media, and the educational system—has been under the thumb of the assholes for so long it will take a major effort to dislodge them. Through bureaucracy, the assholes have become entrenched in government, and are not about to leave willingly. The media stands ready to suppress any news and warnings about the Association—or even assholism. (They pretend that my books and others on assholism just do not exist.) And our schools, through political correctness, have made damned sure that no student is going to develop the analytical skills to detect the existence of the Association all on his or her own.

Nonetheless, human decency still survives—and even thrives in the hearts of good people. As we saw in World War II, there is no force on earth—not even the Super Browns—who can overpower decent people once they see the need to act.

At the same time, it is important to exercise caution. One crusader striking out on his or her own is bound to be destroyed. The assholes are thoroughly entrenched in every major segment of society. The Super Browns have been plotting and planning for centuries to take over the world. They are rapidly closing in on their goal.

Granted, some of their earlier efforts were too overt, and backfired. It is hard for the Association to keep that fierce drive of greed and lust in check, especially among the lesser members of the group. Every once in a while a would-be Hitler or Stalin runs amok, generates a whirlwind of massive destruction, and then is defeated. In these ways, a few highly undisciplined idiots manage to spoil fascism for all assholes. Now they can use it only in religion, business, and social protesting.

Such setbacks should not be taken as signs that the Association is failing to reach its goals. The real work of the Super Browns is far more subtle and clever. Having penetrated and assumed positions of power in all of society's key institutions, they are slowly eroding the very foundation on which we evaluate and understand life. They are castrating the values of freedom and liberty on which this country was founded; they are poisoning the concepts of goodwill and trust upon which any valid religion is based; and they have muddied our perceptions of truth.

This dirty work has gone on right underneath our noses, and yet only a few of us are able to smell the ordure.

One good example is the current drive in many public schools to promote a healthy self-image in all pupils. Obviously, a good self-image is desirable, but this campaign is often taken way too far, where children are taught to feel good about themselves even if they misbehave or perform poorly. This kind of instruction sets them up to a) weaken their conscience so that they become assholes, or b) weaken their intelligence so that they become easy targets for assholes later in life. I can imagine the news reports now:

"The arresting officer asked the boy why he had broken into the 7-11, stolen a box of ice cream bars, and then shot the clerk on the way out.

" 'He wanted me to pay,' the lad answered.

" 'But that's murder! You are a criminal.'

" 'No, I'm not. I'm a wonderful human being.' "

This is a typical little brown trick. They take a healthy concept and gut it of its good contents, repackage it, and then present it as a solution to society's problems. But empty packages make worthless gifts.

The same kind of mind control has occurred in

58

religion. As Arch Bishop puts it in his striking commentary, *Sin in the Sanctuary*, "Fundamentalist Christianity is not really the worship of God or Christ. It is just devil worship disguised as something else. It is primarily *about* the devil, after all— *fearing* the devil, *looking* for the devil, trying to *ward off* the devil, and preparing *to do battle* with the devil. Fundamentalists spend all their time condemning non-believers and threatening them with fear, guilt, loathing, and eternal damnation. At the last minute, then, they throw in the caveat that God will save them if they believe in Him. But 59 minutes worth of assholism cannot be redeemed by one minute of piety. It just doesn't work that way."

Even the Super Browns have been surprised by how readily accepted fundamentalism has been. Their long range plans had called for making radical fundamentalism so outrageous and lacking in charity that decent people would be driven either to atheism or some passive religion that promotes blandness and harmlessness. Either way, they would win.

Actually, fundamentalism has become something of an embarrassment to the assholes, because they know it is only a matter of time before decent human beings wise up to its extremism. Sooner or later, those in authority are going to state that there is no Christ in fundamentalist Christianity, and their shell game will collapse.

Even that will not be much of a setback for the Association, though. They have other plans. In anticipation of that occasion, they have infiltrated mainstream Christianity and stirred up a whirlwind. As counterpoint to the strict moral harshness of fundamentalism, they have driven the mainstream church into a morass of permissiveness and moral laxity. Goodhearted but unsuspecting Christians are now being taught:

• No one really sins. They are just acting out their frustrations as victims of society.

• Morality is whatever you think it is.

• God's nature is somewhere between Santa Claus and the tooth fairy.

• We must share the burden of less fortunate people by feeling guilty about the way we—and our forefathers before us—have exploited and oppressed them.

• The way to God is through a good attendance record at church.

At times, it seems as though a potted geranium could become a good Christian, as long as it kept up its tithe to the church.

The more decent people accept the instruction to be passive, stop thinking, and trust in the church, the more firmly entrenched the asshole's agenda becomes.

In any other context, this pattern would be seen as a formula for exploitation—because it is. Either that, or it's a script for a Mickey Mouse movie.

A profession that is heavily influenced by assholistic beliefs is psychology. This is a science and healing art that is supposed to help people cope with anger, fear, grief, and guilt. But has it done so?

No—because the assholes have taken over.

We are now being told in consulting rooms, in women's magazines, and on TV talk shows that anger is a perfectly healthy emotion. Fear is part of our humanity. It is normal to feel prolonged grief

60

over a major loss. If you do not have personal guilt to carry around, you ought to at least feel guilty about how you have exploited everyone less fortunate. And if you feel happy, it's only because you have suppressed your negativity.

This is unadulterated bullshit—the kind of bullshit that could only come from assholes.

Anger attacks your physical health. Fear clogs up the arteries of your expectations and opportunities. Grief traps you in the past and your own little selfish world. Guilt imprisons you in eternal self-punishment. None of these is desirable.

Instead of being taught how to put the pieces of their shattered lives back together, most people in therapy are taught to chop the pieces even more finely. They are taught to bleed emotionally—to become even angrier by learning to blame almost everyone but themselves for their problems. As a result, they become more and more emotionally unstable—and easier targets for the Association.

Through these and other tactics, the Association has been able to divert the great flow of evolution from its course. Their gains have been subtle, not blatant, for they operate behind the scenes. They operate through mind control, by distorting the basic precepts we believe in and act upon.

It is time to spot these patterns and stop letting assholes dump on us. It only takes one clear voice, heard at the right moment, to expose the assholes at their game. For once the truth is known, they can no longer hide behind their brown veil of confusion and bullshit.

It's time to let the shit hit the fan. Just make sure you are standing behind it.

9
Bobbing for Assholes

A feminist with statistics is like a
fish with a Thigh Master.®
—Bob Henderson

Bob Henderson, an old friend and patient of
mine, was on the phone.

"How the hell are you, Bob?" I asked.

"Not well," he replied. "I feel lower than whale-
shit."

"The assholes get to you?" I asked.

"In spades. I need to talk with you about it."

"Come on over. The afternoon is yours."

So Bob came over. Bob was a first-rate reporter
for a local TV station and a flaming asshole when he
first took my classes. His specialty was beating up
his wife—never anything too messy, but lots and
lots of bruises. Finally, she got smart and took a
hike, leaving Bob to beat up himself. Instead, he
came to me and found out what he should have
known all along: that he was an asshole.

But that was five years ago. After a couple years
in an ANAL group and some pretty intense counseling, Bob discovered the decent human being
within himself. He stopped being abusive and re-

married. In fact, he married a woman who had been kicked around pretty badly in her first marriage. They had met in an ANAL session, where she was learning how not to be a sissy asshole. They've been married three years now.

"How's Annie?" I asked when Bob first arrived. I was afraid that the old patterns were resurfacing, and that was why Bob was so depressed.

"Annie? Oh, she's a doll." He guessed where I was heading. "We're not having any problems," Bob assured me. "Annie's the greatest thing that ever happened to me—other than you."

"Then what's wrong?"

"I've quit my job."

That was a bombshell that blew me away. Bob had become the lead reporter on the biggest TV station in town; he was seriously being considered for an anchor spot the next time the station re-shuffled its image. It was almost unthinkable that Bob would walk away from that opportunity.

"Tell me about it," I said.

"As you probably know, it has been sweeps month," Bob began, "and my producer asked me to do a series of reports on abusive marriages. I was delighted. Between Annie and me, we probably know half of the abused spouses in the city, and all of the experts. This was right up my alley. And something I could really put my heart into. You knew that Annie has been volunteering at a battered women's center, didn't you?"

I nodded yes.

"Anyway, I was really geared up. But I wanted to tell the whole story, not just half of it. As I dug into the story, I found out something startling. Most people think the problem is just one of men beating up women. But it's not. Men get beaten up by their wives, too."

He leaned toward me. "Do you know what the ratio actually is?"

"Of what?"

"Of women being beaten up by their husbands as compared to men being beaten up by their wives?"

"I don't know. I would guess 8 or 9 to one."

"It's actually one to one."

I must have looked startled, because Bob said: "I've seen that reaction before. We think we know these facts, but we don't—not unless we dig real hard for them.

"But you were partly right, though. Women are 8 or 9 times more likely to report abuse than men."

I knew Bob had done his homework—he was one of the most thorough and careful journalists I had ever met. "Well, it makes sense," I replied. "I know one thing for sure. There is the same number of assholes among women as among men. Assholism is not sexist—or racist, for that matter. Neither sex has a monopoly on selfishness, malice, or rudeness."

Bob nodded. "When I was first assigned the story, my boss asked me to be sure to spike it by interviewing some of the better known male bashing feminists. I objected, but he insisted. "It's sweeps, after all," he said. "We want to be sure to raise some eyebrows."

"So I interviewed them, but in the final report, I also included comments from more rational women that basically indicated that the male bashers were grossly distorting the truth with their wild statements and false charges."

"What kind of wild statements?" I asked.

"Well, one of them repeated the old chestnut that wife beatings increase 40 percent on the day of the Super Bowl, and that women's shelters are swamped on that particular day. Hospital emergency rooms are supposed to be deluged with battered women."

"That doesn't make much sense to me," I said. "I would think that men would be so caught up in the game that they would just ignore their wives—not pick a fight with them."

"You are absolutely right. So I interviewed doctors in emergency rooms, the women that staff the shelters, and the police that answer calls of domestic violence. They all reported that activity was unusually calm on Super Sunday. The statistic was just something made up by the male bashers.

"But when the report was aired, all of the inflammatory quotes were left in, and all of the quotes correcting them had been edited out—not by me, but by my boss. And without the courtesy of notifying me in advance.

"In fact, he had actually called up Tish Tush, the president of SNOW (Supreme National Organization for Women), asked her to comment on these inaccuracies, and tacked it on to the end of my story. 'What's an occasional statistical error in the light of the massive injustices women have suffered?' she asked. 'Let's not quibble over such petty details.'

"Can you believe that—petty details? When did journalistic integrity become a petty detail?"

I was tempted to say "about twenty-five years ago, from what I can tell," but I bit my tongue in deference to my friend. He continued:

"I stormed into his office and demanded to know

65

why he had allowed those changes to be made."

" 'Allow them?' he asked. 'I insisted on them.'

" 'But they distort the truth.'

" 'I disagree,' he smiled. 'It presents the truth in a way that advances a good cause—a cause that both you and I support.'

"He was so smooth it was chilling. To my mind, he was committing cold-blooded murder of the journalistic profession right before my eyes.

"So I quit. He made no effort to stop me."

Bob sat there and shook his head. "I know I did the right thing—the only thing I could do. But I feel just awful. I feel as though I've lost grasp of truth."

I didn't know what to say. I was as stunned as Bob was. "You've just had a bucket of slime dumped on you by a very accomplished asshole. It is normal to feel as you do. What you did was absolutely right. Don't let the asshole get you down."

At that moment, the room suddenly became quite cold. The sensation was intense—and distinctly uncomfortable. I turned back to Bob.

"Did your boss ever mention the Association?"

Bob gasped. "How did you know?"

"I'm an expert on assholes," I smiled.

"It was after I quit. He shook his head slightly, made a little sigh, and then said, 'And I thought you might be good material for the Association. But I was wrong—you couldn't even pass the first test.' I had no idea what he was talking about."

"It doesn't matter," I said. "I'm not sure about it all myself. But there is one thing you can be sure of. You didn't fail the test—you passed it. With flying colors. I'm proud of you, Bob. You really aren't an asshole anymore."

66

Part Three:
Assholes, Then and Now

10

In the Beginning, There Were Assholes

Two words you should never believe: "Trust me."
—*Dr. Crement's Pocket Guide To Surviving Assholism*

No one knows exactly when the Association was first formed. I suspect it was when one Neanderthal became jealous of another and spread rumors that he was a vegetarian. Some speculate that it must have been in the Garden of Eden—or at least when Cain murdered Abel. But I doubt it. Assholes are past masters at using Biblical stories to promote their own nonsense—and fill us with fear and shame.

We can, however, trace the beginnings of the asshole conspiracy at least as far back as the doctrine of original sin, a classic example of assholism at work. The underlying precept of original sin is that we are all damned forever for something none of us did. It is a complete distortion of the teachings of Jesus, and yet was accepted as dogma by the Church

68

hundreds of years ago. As a result, the Western world has suffered under an impossible burden of guilt ever since.

Who voted to accept this pernicious doctrine on our behalf?

It wasn't me. Was it you?

Of course not. It was assholes!

In fact, the use of original sin to spread guilt typifies the way assholes "share" things with the rest of us. If it is something we might benefit from, they will ban it. But if it something that might ruin our lives, they let us have as much as we want. Indeed, they insist on it.

This, incidentally, is the way assholes practice atonement—they simply make the rest of us feel as badly as they do. Or worse. This is also what the asshole believes is the democratic process. Make everyone suffer equally.

Of course, most of the early examples of assholism have been lost to history, not just because they occurred a long time ago but also because assholes are adroit at covering their rears. Nonetheless, history still records plenty of obvious cases, as in the lives and exploits of:

Attila the Hun.

Joseph Stalin.

Adolph Hitler.

Mao Tse Tung.

Each of these is a monstrous example of the asshole abuse of power, combining rudeness, destructiveness, disrespect for others, the lust for power, and ignorance in one massive asshole. But as perfect as each of these assholes was, it is clear that they did not act alone. They could only have ascended to power and remained there if they were supported by thousands of lesser assholes. In other words, these regimes were times when the usually secret Association became visible. And yet, because the regimes all eventually collapsed, the rest of us missed the obvious: these governments were totally controlled by assholes.

This is not a point to be dismissed lightly. Stalin and Hitler inflicted massive wounds upon their people, but some of their lieutenants were even more vicious and vindictive than they. Lots of lesser assholes had free rein during these reigns to scheme, connive, oppress, exploit, pillage, and annihilate. These posts were rewards for years of faithful, unquestioning service in the labors of the Association.

Power in any form is always a tremendous lure for the aspiring asshole—and total power, as in the control of a whole country, is irresistible. This is the reason why so many assholes rushed to serve as bishops, archbishops, and popes during the Middle Ages—and why the same type of person now seeks out careers in law and government.

While power is an undeniable lure, money and sex are also important motivators for assholes. But these usually come along with power. Witness the great debauchery of the Romans in their heyday, which was almost as complete as that of modern American senators and evangelists.

But history reveals something else about assholes, if we are alert enough to spot it. Assholes seek to destroy everything that a) they don't understand—such as truth, justice, cooperation, honesty, and kindness—and b) stands in their way, namely the rest of us.

In fact, in the archives of the Association, an ancient creed cites truth, honesty, and justice as the "evil triumvirate"—the three things all assholes must fear above all else. All assholes are pledged to work to stamp out truth, honesty, and justice where-ever they find it. *This is their primary assignment!*

After all, what is more dangerous to a fraud than the truth?

What is more embarrassing to a con artist than honesty?

What is more dangerous to a crook than justice?

Wisdom is also a terrible threat to assholes. This is why they engineered the destruction of the great library at Alexandria—a library that was said to contain the full sum of human knowledge up to that point. The loss of this library was a tremendous setback to the intellectual development of human-ity. It was a major victory for the Association.

The Association tried the same thing at the on-set of the Renaissance, using fear and their influ-ence in the Church—and the machinery of the Inquisition—to arrest and convict such great minds as Galileo on charges of heresy.

What great sin had Galileo committed? He had proven that Aristotle and Ptolemy were wrong—that the earth revolved about the sun, rather than the other way around. This troubled the assholes in the church, who had long perpetuated this false teaching as a way of keeping the public in chains of ignorance. So, even though Galileo had published his famous treatise under the imprimatur of the Pope, he was convicted of heresy on the basis of a planted letter—a common little brown trick. He spent the last eight years of his life confined by

71

house arrest. Fortunately, Galileo's work was picked up and extended by great minds that were out of the reach of the church's great assholes. Once his ideas were commonly accepted, the assholes had to back down.

Some people (probably assholes themselves) may be inclined to scoff at this one example, dismissing it as an aberration of a superstitious time. But the story of Galileo may be more sinister than it first appears. Who kept the best minds of Europe in ignorance for fifteen hundred years about these simple astronomical truths—and many other truths as well? Who would ever be afraid of discovering the truth about any aspect of life?

Could it be a conspiracy of assholes?

Just who decided for us that we already knew everything we needed to know?

Who decided that the opinions of a few self-righteous bigots were more important than the facts?

And who voted to make maintaining the status quo more important than the search for truth and discovery?

It was assholes then—just as it is assholes now. We must learn the lessons that history teaches us, for they will be repeated—are being repeated—until we learn them. Until we kick ass and discredit this insidious conspiracy.

11
Learning the Hard Way

> If you receive a ticking package in
> the mail, do not open it. It may be a
> love note from an asshole.
> —*Dr. Crement's Pocket Guide To
> Surviving Assholism*

There are many lessons history teaches us about
assholes, once we open our eyes and learn to see.

First and foremost among these is war, easily the
greatest invention ever of the asshole conspiracy.
Decent human beings would always rather settle
disputes amicably than risk a violent confrontation.
War is not in their nature. But assholes, being
blinded by greed and their lust for power, are
always eager to go to war. They care little about the
risk of being killed—or the fact that thousands of
people will lose their lives and property. They smell
profit and power, and will not be deterred.

War is always a sign that decent leadership has
failed, and the assholes have taken over. In some
wars, like World War II, the crisis is precipitated by
the aggressiveness of one side—i.e., the Axis (which
probably ought to be renamed the Asses). The

73

decent human beings on the other side—the Allies—had no option but to fight back and defend themselves.

This was also the pattern in other unnecessary wars, such as the Crusades. These were wars that were sponsored by an unholy alliance of the assholes in European government and religion at the time. Faced with difficult problems at home, the monarchs and priests decided the best solution was to shift attention away from these problems by attacking the "infidel." The infidel, it turned out, were Arabs living in Jerusalem.

Europe had no more claim to Jerusalem than a gnat does, but logic is never required in the campaigns of assholes. And so a succession of wars were launched to liberate the Holy City of its rightful inhabitants, at the cost of many lives on both sides.

The striking characteristic of the Crusades is that it enjoined good people to kill other good people, temporarily known as infidels, in the hope of pleasing God. This is an assholistic concept through and through. Decent people innately know that God is a God of Love, and does not encourage us to go around killing one another. War is an abomination to God, but sweet music to the ears of assholes.

In some wars, the assholes are in charge of both camps. This is usually the case in civil strife. In Ireland, Catholic assholes bomb Protestant assholes, while the decent human beings cower in the background and pray for peace. In the Middle East, Palestinian assholes terrorize Israeli assholes, and vice-versa. Unfortunately, innocent people often get caught in the crossfire.

When will such nonsense end? Only when the

assholes kill each other off, and sanity can return to the scene.

Some strife simmers and boils just below the surface of society, never breaking out into full-scale war. A good example of this would be the Inquisition, that most unholy campaign of the Catholic Church to rid its ranks of heresy, and to impose purity through torture. The Inquisition is dramatic proof that no one can be a meaner sonofabitch than an asshole posing as a cleric. Indeed, the abuse of power by the Inquisitors makes 20th century malice and mischief look like child's play in comparison.

The Inquisitors claimed to derive their authority from God; they wrapped themselves in the cloak of protecting truth. But to discover this truth, they tortured good people. To save their souls, they hanged and burned their bodies. To serve their God, they stole property and destroyed careers.

This is not the work of enlightened people. It is the work of assholes!

Slavery is another institution that was obviously the work of the Association. The Greeks practiced it. Africans (before they were known as Afro-Americans) practiced it. In this country, the South practiced it until the North dissuaded them.

Slavery is exploitation without restrictions. It reduces a human being to a piece of property to be controlled—and even killed—by another human being. Decent human beings are appalled at such systems. Members of the asshole conspiracy, on the other hand, consider it one of their most brilliant inventions—and mourn its passing from the world scene.

What we need to understand is that the decent

people of slaveholding societies were never the ones who suggested it, voted for it, or supported it. Slavery was always imposed—both on the slaves and society. Wherever slavery was an institution, it was assholes who promoted it.

Another great invention of assholes—and a problem that still creates terrible mischief in society—is Puritanism. The asshole's hideous hypocrisy and intense rage against decent behavior is embodied in the precepts and practices of the Puritans.

The Puritans believed that one could only find joy in a life of misery and joylessness. So they forbade fashionable clothes, music, dancing, card-playing, drinking, and the reading of almost anything other than the Bible. In a day before the existence of television or radio, that did not leave much to do. Laughter was frowned on. Swearing or cursing was verboten. If they had known about golf, they would have banned that, too.

Reasonable people do not deny themselves the pleasures of life to this extreme. Without embracing hedonism, they learn that it is possible to use leisure activities and pleasures to enrich life, making it more satisfying and fulfilling. Only assholes would propose such a system with a straight face—not for themselves, of course, but for all the rest of us.

The Puritans taught that duty was first and foremost. Everything else had to be sacrificed to the performance of duty.

But who got to decide what duty was—and was not? Not the ordinary members of the congregation. No—it was those damned assholes again.

In many ways, Puritanism exemplifies how the

asshole conspiracy works. A few assholes seize power in a group and then proceed to issue new rules and procedures. First, they define the difference between right and wrong, and then they declare that almost everything is wrong! Even virtues such as cheerfulness are inverted, becoming something nasty and unclean that must be purged. Impoverishment of the personality life is defined as the true way to enrich the life of spirit.

Would decent people ever consent to such ludicrous practices? Of course not. First, they must be brainwashed by the assholes.

Having seen through and repudiated the nonsensical dogma of Puritanism, it is easy to see it as the handiwork of the Super Browns. But it is a lot more difficult to see these patterns while you are still immersed in their propaganda and lies. This is because the Association has made great strides in learning how to confuse and suppress rational thought *before* they launch one of their crazy schemes. This guarantees that they will be able to implement it without much opposition.

The ready acceptance of Marxist theories and principles by the intelligentsia of this country is a perfect example of this suppression of rational thought. A cursory review of the principles of Karl Marx should leave a sensible person rolling on the floor with laughter. Marx's dialectic is so full of loopy ideas that it does not merit serious consideration. Marxism claims to promote a classless society, for instance, but simultaneously advocates the ultimate in class warfare! It wraps itself in a pious cloak of "economic justice," but then proposes stealing property from its owners as the way to enforce this justice.

77

Despite the absurdity of these ideas, Marxism has been widely accepted. Whenever it has been tried as an economic system in dozens of countries, it has failed miserably. Yet otherwise intelligent people in virtually every college in this nation still cling to it. Why? Because the spell of bullshit that the Association has woven to seduce these people is still strong. These people have not yet awakened and learned that they are walking in Mao's dung.

Assholes know that their schemes and proposals never really make sense, if subjected to intelligent scrutiny. So they know they must confuse us—distract us from looking too closely at their evidence or proof. Once the cover is blown on one hoax, they will move quickly onto the next. In this way, they are fairly successful in keeping the rest of us guessing.

Another favorite little brown trick is to disguise their lust for power by advancing themselves as "reformers." To distract us from the opportunism and shallowness of their plans, they advertise their noble motives, the suffering of the masses, the crushing need for justice, the gravity of the threat, the repulsiveness of the people (usually non-assholes) who are presently in power, and the urgent need to do something *right now.*

Sounds like a page from the script of a modern politician, doesn't it?

The assholes are still with us, alive and well.

In Washington, D.C.

In New York City.

In Los Angeles.

In your town and mine.

They are writing—and maybe even rewriting—the pages of history.

12
Undercover Among The Assholes

Once you win their minds and hearts,
the rest of them follows, too.
—Mao's little red book

I had encouraged Joe—remember Joe?—to stay at his university and continue his quest for tenure. I thought it would be valuable for him to pretend to be the protégé of his asshole superior—it would let him go undercover among the assholes and discover the truth about their modus operandi.

I didn't hear from him for several months, until one morning when a packet arrived at my office by next day delivery. It was from Joe, and it contained a microcassette recording he had apparently made clandestinely while attending a meeting of professors who belonged to the Association.

Joe was being indoctrinated into the inner circle. The first voice spoke of the need for discretion:

"Not everyone understands our goals and methods," he said. "So we must be careful whom we talk with. A lot of people who sound like us might recoil if they learned of our agenda. So it is best to keep these things a secret. And it goes without saying that we should never refer to the Association, except among ourselves."

"Couldn't we spread our ideas more rapidly if we went public with them?" Joe asked.

"Oh, no—never," the first voice replied. "It is our job to take the complex issues of our day and simplify them so that even college students can understand them."

Yes, I thought—that is always the rationale the arrogant use to talk down to everyone else. They figure that they are the only ones smart enough to understand life, and they certainly aren't going to share what they know with others. Instead, they reduce it to pablum—half-thoughts that let them exploit and control the thinking of whoever is dumb enough to listen. So, this is what happens when assholism is merged with professorial elitism—it becomes bullshit with a degree!

Other voices picked up the indoctrination. "All information is inherently political; all knowledge forces people to take sides, advocating one set of ideas and excluding others. Here at the university, we have an incredible opportunity to mold minds to be receptive to our particular way of viewing the world—to fight injustice, recognize the terrible wrongs that exist in society, and promote reform. This is all we are doing. We are organizing the thinking of our students to support our goals. And the beauty of it all is that this can be done as easily in a math or music class as in a philosophy seminar."

Joe asked how it could be done in a math class.

"Easy," the voice replied. "You pose math problems based on the pitiful hourly wages that the oppressed earn. You can teach ratios by showing how the earning power of those wages steadily decline. In this way, you prepare the student to accept the portrait of life in this country we will paint for him in other classes."

"Isn't that rather blatant?" Joe asked. "I'm not a math teacher, but I should think the students wouldn't let someone get away with that."

A third voice spoke up. "Not if they want a good grade, they don't." There was general laughter on the tape—but I wasn't laughing. I didn't hear Joe laughing, either.

A woman continued the discussion. "I suppose you think it's a bit exploitative and unfair to lead students in this way. But keep in mind that society itself is unjust and exploitative. How can we feel that we have prepared our students for life unless they are able to see this about society?"

"Why don't we just teach people to think calmly and rationally and make up their own minds?" I heard Joe ask.

There followed such a crush of voices that I thought Babel had fallen again. At least five people were talking—probably arguing—all at the same time. Finally, a female voice broke through and spoke in angry tones:

"We *do* want people to think, of course, but there are various levels of refinement in thinking. We don't leave our students alone to choose the curriculum they are to study, do we? Of course not. They wouldn't know what to read. It is our duty as professors to assign their curriculum. It is also our duty to shape and mold their thinking to match the realities of our culture and times.

"You *do* agree with us that government is not doing enough to help the disadvantaged, that big business exploits the poor, and that power must be returned to the people, don't you? That's why you were chosen for this group, you know."

"Yes, I know," Joe said. "And I concur completely with these positions." Actually, I knew that Joe's thinking was undergoing a major evolution since he discovered that these thoughts had actually been implanted by assholes. But he was in no position to openly change his tune now. So he hummed along.

"But what exactly is this group I am joining? Is it part of some larger association? Or is this all there is?"

This question hit the mother lode. No asshole wants to be perceived as being part of an insignificant group or movement.

"The Association is a very large organization that operates worldwide. There isn't a college campus anywhere, in any country, that doesn't have a group of agents such as ourselves hard at work.

"There isn't a newspaper or TV network that does not have agents of the Association in key executive positions.

"There isn't a major corporation that is not influenced and directed by the Association—and the same can be said for the labor unions.

"There isn't a government bureaucracy anywhere that makes a decision without first clearing it through the Association.

"So you can see, we wield a great deal of power. We are visionaries who are bonded together by the common goals and ideals we share. We are the vanguard of a new era of peace and understanding."

"I think that's great," Joe said. "Why can't you do it without brainwashing students? Why don't you just lay out your programs instead of harping so much on the corruption, injustice, and greed? Let the students sort it out for themselves."

It was the angry woman again. "Trust me—we know what we are doing. Promoting good works just lulls the public into optimism. To motivate them, you have to whip them into a frenzy of rage and outrage. Unless the public is full of grievances, confusion, and despair, it is hard to keep their attention. We have to motivate them."

"Now I understand," Joe said.

So did I. The halls of ivy should be called the halls of assademia—not academia.

ASSHOLE FORCES IN SOCIETY

1. Political correctness.
2. Proposed universal health care.
3. The abortion debate—get a life, everyone.
4. Beavis and Butthead.
5. Credit bureaus.
6. The need for metal detectors in schools.
7. The controversy over gays in the military.
8. Male bashing.
9. Male bonding.
10. Mail service.
11. Ellen Goodperson.
12. Quotas.
13. Task forces.
14. Punk rock.
15. Welfare.
16. Welfare fraud.
17. Welfare reform.
18. The NRA.
19. Nintendo.
20. Book banning and burning.
21. Dr. Jack Kervorkian.
22. Reenactments of the Civil War.
23. The Anita Hill phenomenon.
24. Lobbies.
25. The whole idea of co-dependency.
26. Tabloid TV shows.
27. The IRS.
28. Phony deficit cutting.
29. People who believe in conspiracies.
30. People who think "asshole" is vulgar.

Part Four:
Vandals
of the Mind

13
Sucked to Death

> Once you know how assholes work, encountering one is something like being sucked into the vortex of a tornado. You know there's nothing there, but you cannot help being pulled in.
> —Jasmine Lark in *The Grass is Always Brown After A Visit from an Asshole*

Joseph Goebbels, Adolph Hitler's minister of proaganda and one of the Association's hall of fame members, was fond of saying that the bigger the lie, the easier it was to confuse people with it. This is also true of how we relate to events. We can grasp the reality of a friend dying in an automobile accident, for instance, but find it hard to comprehend that a half million people have died in a revolution in some Third World nation.

In much the same way, it is easy to detect rudeness and exploitation at the individual level, but much harder to see when whole institutions or groups are behaving like assholes. Yet, once we decent human beings begin to recognize the tell-tale signs of an asshole conspiracy, we must make the effort to expand our vision—or resign ourselves to smelling assholes the rest of our lives!

It is not just the huge scale of the asshole conspiracy that is hard to detect, but also the subtlety of its methods. Always keep in mind that given the chance to be honest or be devious, the asshole will always choose deviousness, as it gives him a greater thrill. For this reason, the asshole is also highly accomplished in covering his rear—and in fact often knows how he will blame the outcome of his efforts on someone else even before he knows just what it is he is going to do!

Decent human beings, by contrast, will always choose to be honest. For this reason, we automatically fail to suspect the deviousness of assholes, until it is too late.

Unless, of course, we learn to spot assholes.

Ben Masterson expands on this theme in his landmark book, *Sucked to Death by Assholes*.

"The saddest thing of all," he writes, "is that we often do not comprehend that we have been sucked dry by an asshole until it is all over. Suddenly, we realize that we have done someone else's work or taken the fall for someone else's incompetence. And worse, we did it all with our eyes open—but unable to see. Only after we get stuck again and again do we finally catch on that we are being used. And use us they do. When we finally object, they launch into a long lecture about how pathetic their situation is and how cruel it is for us to refuse them the tiny bit of friendship they are begging for. Begging, hell! They are just sucking us to death, and we are permitting them to do it. We are willingly opening our minds and hearts—and maybe our pocket-books, too—and letting them guzzle away.

"There's only one way to stop the loss. We have to stand up to the asshole and unsuck ourselves!"

Let this be our motto then: Unsuck yourself. Not just from friends and colleagues who happen to be assholes, but also from the larger influences of ass-holism in society. The welfare problem does not exist in this country just because the assholes have controlled the government bureaucracy for years. Far more importantly, it exists because decent Americans have been suckered into believing that a) it is necessary and b) it is actually solving a social problem. We continue to believe this even though the evidence has existed for decades that welfare is making worse the social problems it was designed to solve. It has created generation after generation of people who are addicted to the dole. But welfare will never be changed by our government—it is packed with assholes! Before any meaningful re-form can occur, decent Americans must unsuck themselves from their belief in the welfare system.

Welfare is just one way in which governmental assholes are sucking us to death. To expand our vision properly, we must become aware of them all, and put a halt to our end of the con. We must unsuck ourselves from the desire to be cared for by the government.

Many of these cons, both in government and in the rest of society, are very slick examples of leger-demain. Just as an embezzler is not going to tell his co-workers that he plans to slip $500,000 of the corporate funds into his own bank accounts over the next two years, conspiring assholes do not take out full page ads in the Sunday paper to announce their devious plots and activities. I wish it were that simple!

In reality, society has been slowly brainwashed into accepting premises it would never have accepted fifty or one hundred years ago. This, in turn, has altered how we think about major issues—and even curtailed the scope of our vision. In this way, the assholes have gained control of our minds.

Once the mind is theirs, all that is left is to hook up the hoses and start sucking.

They suck out all of our cherished values and virtues, and replace them with situational ethics.

They suck out our strength and courage and replace them with permissiveness and passiveness.

They suck out our idealism and replace it with acceptance of the status quo.

They suck out our sense of responsibility and replace it with a demand for entitlements.

What proof do I have of this? The daily newspaper in any American city is proof enough.

Remember when it was considered honorable to earn your own living and make a good income? When a self-made man or woman was a hero? Nowadays, self-made people are suspected of being crooks or scoundrels, for they must have made their fortunes exploiting the poor. And growing segments of society believe that it is silly to work when you can be on welfare. Do you remember voting to make these changes in our thinking? Who made them?

Assholes, of course, by brainwashing the American public.

Remember when it was a terrible disgrace to

have a baby out of wedlock? When did it become all right to have babies without husbands? Who said it was acceptable?

Assholes, of course, by undermining commonly-held American values.

Remember when entertainment did not include puking on stage, smashing guitars, and exposing your genitals? Who decided that repulsiveness could be entertaining? Did you vote on it? Who warped the minds of our youth?

Assholes, of course.

Remember when people dressed up before going out in public, as a courtesy to one another? Who decided that grunge was desirable—even fashionable? When did it become okay to look and smell like a slob? Do you recall voting for this? Then how could these social attitudes change so drastically?

Was it assholes? You bet your untied running shoes it was.

Society, too, has been sucked dry by the assholes—by the deliberate efforts of the Association. But it is not just the overt changes in our lifestyle that are the most troubling. The real problem is the unseen vandalism which is occurring in our thinking—the trashing of our thoughts and minds individually, as well as the pillaging and looting of our social values and standards collectively.

It is as though some punk had taken a can of spray paint and marked swastikas on our front door, and we just sat at home, immobile. Most of us wouldn't dream of letting this vandalism stand. We would remove the paint and try to apprehend the vandals. But we are not taking that kind of action when it comes to the vandalism of society. We have let our standards of decency be smeared with graffiti. We have let our principles and ideals be mugged by thugs. We have stood by and watched our family values be trashed.

Oddly enough, it would not take much to reverse the trend—just a few decent people who are willing to call an asshole an asshole.

As we encounter assholes in government, religion, business, the media, the entertainment industry, or education, we need to write to them and tell them that we have caught on.

We know they are assholes.

For maximum impact, send them a copy of this book. Let them know you are not going to be bamboozled anymore.

And add one more message—that you expect them to undo all the mischief they have done; to repair all of the damage they have caused.

Tell them:

"It's your mess—you clean it up."

14
The Big Lie
ASSHOLISM IN GOVERNMENT

> When a politician comes to town,
> watch your wallet.
> —A retired asshole fighter

Does the long arm of the Association extend into government? Is the Pope Catholic?

Once upon a time in America, we had a government "of the people, by the people, and for the people." In the century and a half since Abraham Lincoln coined this phrase, we have largely exchanged our democracy for what can only be called an "ass-ocracy"—a government of the assholes, by the assholes, and for the assholes.

I still fondly believe that the day will come when we will rid the government of the parasitic assholes who make it their home. But that would take either an act of God or an act of the awakened citizenry. Of the two, the act of God is probably the more reasonable.

This is not because the people do not care, but because they have been seduced by the big lie. When it comes to government, there are several big lies:

- That our modern government has to be BIG.
- That our government has to be expensive.
- That the bureaucracy that runs government cannot be trimmed.
- That entitlement programs cannot be cut.

How have we come to believe these lies? We have been brainwashed by assholes.

Not all politicians or bureaucrats are assholes, of course, but the stink created by those who are permeate the whole government. The brown haze that hangs over Washington, D.C. isn't smog, you know—it is the obfuscating fog of bullshit.

Actually, government is tailor made for assholes. In politics, an essential step to getting elected is campaigning. And what is campaigning other than a massive assault of assholism upon the intelligence of the voting public? Campaigning is the art of making promises you have little intention of keeping, disowning values and principles you used to have if they might offend someone, and lulling the public into believing you are the best candidate.

In this kind of forum, an asshole will beat a decent person every time—unless he shoots himself in the foot.

In some cases, it can even be revealed during the campaign that the candidate has cheated on his wife, not once but many times; that he used influence to avoid the draft; and that he is suspected of shady dealings—and still get elected. Indeed, some candidates for office in this country have managed to win after having been convicted of a felony!

Yes, in this country, any boy or girl can grow up to become President—if he or she has the support of the assholes!

Once elected, asshole characteristics still serve the politician. After all, there is money to be made in government—deals to be cut, bribes to be accepted, campaign funds to be misdirected, and influence to be peddled. These are all special abilities that assholes possess in abundance. Decent human beings, on the other hand, haven't the foggiest idea how to go about demanding a bribe or payoff!

The greatest need of a politician for asshole habits, though, occurs if and when he is caught in some improper activity. This is when the ability to cover one's rear is paramount. The capacity to stand before the press and deny accusations that you know to be perfectly true is something that a decent human being just can't do. Only an asshole can do it.

If anything, the opportunities for assholism to flourish in the bureaucracy are even better. The potential for fraud, deceit, and bribery are about the same as in politics, but the bureaucrats have one big advantage: they are appointed rather than elected. Therefore, the public never gets to judge their *qualifications* for office. In addition, since bureaucrats don't have to run for re-election, the public never gets to judge their *performance,* either. They can hide behind civil service protection in almost every situation.

Even the most petty bureaucrat can therefore treat the citizens he or she serves as dirt to be ground underfoot—and get away with it. It is almost bliss for the petty asshole.

How did we let politics and government end up in this bloated state, dominated by assholes? This is a most curious question to ask—and a startling one to try to answer.

- Just when did we decide that we wanted tons and tons of red tape?

- Just when did we decide that we wanted every second of our life dictated by government regulations, even to the point of dictating which condoms are safe to use?

- Just when did we decide that we wanted government to tax more than half of our income?

- Just when did we decide that we wanted the office of our elected representatives to be run by staffs of dozens of unelected assistants? Aren't we paying our congressmen to do this? Why do we need to pay so many others to do their work for them?

We didn't—and we don't. The assholes made up our minds for us.

It happens all the time. The assholes generate a huge fuss about some simple but annoying problem, such as consumer protection or health care. It may even be a problem we never knew existed, until the assholes defined it for us. But suddenly, even though we have been managing well for years without governmental help, the assholes turn the problem into an urgent crisis.

This is what the assholes call "education." We are being educated about problems we didn't know existed.

Having caught our attention, they now charge the issue with strong emotions. The problem we never knew existed suddenly becomes "a great evil" that is about to destroy us. This is meant to induce not only panic but also guilt—that we have neglected this terrible problem for so long.

Of course, the assholes have no solution for the newly-defined problem. They are just using it for its propaganda value—and to get elected and re-elected. When pressed by the media or constituents for a solution, the asshole politico will suddenly lapse into platitudes and vagueness. He has "a plan" that will do the trick—but he is not yet able to reveal what this plan is.

The one thing you can be sure of—it is going to cost taxpayers a bundle of money.

Have you ever wondered why political solutions always cost taxpayers more money, and never save any?

Is it the rising cost of government programs—or just the rising tide of assholes?

If the asshole politician gets elected on his phony platform, and he is pressed to take action to solve the problem everyone now wants solved, he does not panic. Being an asshole, he knows how to act. He appoints a task force (of assholes with degrees) to study the issue and then report back to him. This prolongs the agony at least a year or two—and is a great way to use the government to pay back political favors accumulated over the years.

Naturally, once the report is done, the politician will never read it. He will give it to his speech-writer to review and find passages that can be easily distorted or misquoted to support his previously formed conclusion. The result is a person of medi-ocre intelligence and less altruism offering saga-cious opinions about issues he knows nothing about—and he supports them with the authority of his task force's report.

How is the average citizen supposed to know that this is all just a con?

Personally, I think the one freedom our forefathers forgot to put in the Bill of Rights was freedom from assholes. It's just as well, however, or the assholes probably would have found a way to get around it, too.

In this way, we have slowly come to believe in the assholes' lies about our government: that it has to be big, that we have to spend more money, and a gargantuan bureaucracy is just the price we pay for all the services government performs. These alone are enough to let the assholes continue to dominate all phases of government. But there is one more big lie that is the biggest of them all:

Government can and should solve all of our problems!

Convincing the public that this big lie is actually true has been the victory of the millenium for the Association. For one thing, it is the exact opposite of what our Founding Fathers believed; as such, it subverts the Constitution in ways that nothing else could. It also lets the assholes justify all manner of other horrible actions—intervening in our lives, taxing us more heavily, loading us down with larger deficits, and stealing our freedoms.

The problem is a somber one. Once you assume that the government can and should fix all problems, then you allow it to arbitrate all differences. Whenever we have a conflict, therefore, we look to the courts or to Congress for a solution. It would never occur to us to work things out amicably, on our own.

When a river floods and wipes out hundreds of homes built too close to the banks, it is no longer the fault of the people who built their homes there. It is the fault of the government, for letting it rain—or for not building better dams. So the President declares it a "federal disaster area" and opens the Treasury vaults to pay for reconstruction. But just who pays the tab? Is it the President? Oh, no. It's you and me.

There's no such thing as an act of God anymore.

Even in something as personal as a car wreck, the asshole specter of our government is always there, hovering. Someone or something must be blamed—the automobile manufacturer, for making an unsafe car; the town, for not erecting traffic signals; or the bartender that served you drinks. Regardless of the circumstances, someone has to be held accountable and forced to pay. Our paternalistic government is there to figure out a) who to blame and b) how much it will cost them.

There's also no such thing as an accident anymore. Just the acts of assholes.

I wouldn't be surprised if some government agency has issued regulations on when it is proper for an American citizen to pick his or her nose. In all likelihood, it requires filing for a permit and completing an environmental study before you may do so. Of course, if you offend anyone while picking your nose, your permit will be immediately rescinded, and you must cancel all further nose picking plans.

Because we have accepted the Super Big Lie, that government can solve all of our problems, we likewise accept—without much question or protest, even—the idea of entitlements. This is the idea that government must guarantee a certain standard of living for retired folks, for welfare mothers, and for the unemployed.

Who pays for these entitlements? The taxpayer.

Who gets to take credit for phony compassion for the poor and the elderly by spending our money?

The asshole politicians.

It doesn't make much sense, does it?

This situation is the demonic creation of the assholes in government. The result is a self-sustaining bureaucratic monster that can only do two things:

1. Demand to be fed more money and power.

2. Crap all over us.

But wait. With assholes, one bad mess always leads to a worse bad mess. Having been encouraged to believe that government can solve all our problems, we now expect our politicians to come up with instant solutions to everything!

This is a formula for certain disaster, but no one seems to notice—or care. The media is preoccupied with lusting for the power that the politicians have. The beneficiaries of the entitlements cheerfully cash their checks every month, not understanding how much they are undermining our democracy as they do it. They do not understand that it's just a monthly bribe for their vote from the assholes in power.

We can be sure of one thing: relief will never come from the assholes. They are the ones who created the problem.

We must therefore decide, as a nation, to stop taking these bribes. We must resume responsibility for our actions, and stop trying to affix blame on others for every unpleasantry that occurs.

Above all, we must start thinking again. We must reclaim our minds and stop letting the assholes trash our rights and values. Our government has been hijacked by a bunch of assholes, and decent people need to recognize this fact and stop letting them get away with it.

Gomer Phyle, in his *Confessions of a Department Head,* reveals how the attitude of the government is often opposed to the interests of the citizen. He writes: "Taxes are a burden to the ordinary schmuck out there, but it is *income* to us. We can't get enough. And what freedoms are still left to the ordinary citizen is just territory we have not yet occupied. But we will."

This principle is confirmed by such asshole theorists as Robert Rake, author of the books *Undermining America's Business* and *The Power of Asshole Ideas:* "The government cannot expect to operate efficiently until it is seizing one hundred percent of the taxpayer's income through taxes. I know it will be hard to convince the public that government needs this money. But we've done the impossible in the past; I see no reason why we cannot do it again in the future. We'll just tell them we're going to make their wages an entitlement."

Haven't we heard the whine of the assholes more than enough?

15
The Brown Fog
ASSHOLISM IN THE MEDIA

> I must admit: you've managed to capture the whole asshole—everything but the stink!
> —Managing editor chewing out a cub reporter for not smearing a person in his story enough.

If government is the perfect refuge for assholes, then the media must be their best friend. In fact, I am not alone in believing that the electronic and print media is just one big public relations arm for the Association. When a member of the Association snaps his fingers and says "Jump," the media asks, "How high?"

The proof is everywhere around us, in our daily newspapers, nightly TV news, and the more popular newsmagazines. Once upon a time, the "news" was a balanced diet of humanity's successes and its tragedies. I can remember, as a little boy, my parents showing me the newspaper clippings of Charles Lindbergh flying solo across the Atlantic. Now, the only kind of story that dominates the papers is the latest scandal about some celebrity or another.

On the whole, the good news is gone—overlooked in favor of messages of doom and disaster, to which we are relentlessly exposed. The media doesn't report that 94 percent of the work force is employed full-time; it reports that 6 percent are unemployed! It would be the same fact in either case, but the first option would emphasize the virtue of the work ethic and the healthiness of the economy, whereas the second option—the one thrust down our throats—reinforces the idea that the government controls everything, and suggests that the economy is not so hot.

The shaping of the news in these ways has become a deliberate effort to make sure we get our daily dose of despair and pessimism. When asked about this slanting, the media apologists always explain that readers just don't want to read about good things. They want all the news, as long as it is rotten.

Tell that to the millions of Americans who still have clippings of Neil Armstrong landing on the moon.

There are far more good news stories out there than rotten ones. It is just that the Association does not want us to start believing that life is pretty good—that we do not need their special assistance.

When a media watchdog group polled the public recently about modern news coverage, 75 percent said they were dissatisfied with the quality of news and how it was reported. In addition, 15 percent actually said they had given up entirely on TV and radio as a source of news, because it was so relentlessly negative. As one respondent, a minister, said,

"To hell with it. I just don't watch TV news anymore. I figure if they shoot the Pope or Wall Street crashes, someone will come over to the house and let me know about it."

Eighty years ago, in the heyday of the daily newspaper, the term "yellow journalism" was coined to describe opportunistic, sleazy reporting. It was a terrible insult to any reporter or editor. Nowadays, the term has disappeared from use—because every newspaper, magazine, and TV news show has stooped to yellow journalism. In fact, they have openly embraced it. Instead of the straight reporting of the facts, we now have commentary printed as news. Instead of a retelling of the bare facts, we have what is euphemistically called "advocacy journalism." It is yellow, through and through.

How does the media respond to these charges? Mostly by howling and crying "foul." Then, like the assholes most of them are, they blur the question with a non-answer, protesting that they go to great lengths to provide balance to major news stories.

This is what I call "truth in assholism." Having been accused of substituting their own opinions for facts, they shift issues and brag about how balanced their reporting is. But balance to a journalist is a slippery proposition. In a recent story about the Ku Klux Klan, for example, the "balance" was provided by interviewing a lieutenant of a radical black militant. In a TV debate about AIDS care, a gay activist represented one point of view, while a fanatical right-wing evangelist presented the other.

These presentations are about as balanced as the *Lusitania* after it had been hit by German torpedos. Or the federal budget.

I am certain that if World War II had occurred today, Eva Braun and Rachele Mussolini would have been invited onto the *Donahue* and *Geraldo* shows, to lend balance to our view of their controversial "significant others." We would have been shown the "human side" of Adolph and Benito, and how they were the kindest, sweetest men in the world, greatly misunderstood outside of their own countries.

This is not balance—it's bullshit. It is brown propaganda serving the asshole cause. And once the basic facts of a story are presented in a biased, distorted way, there is nothing much you can do to restore "balance." It's gone with the wind. Assholes know that most retractions go unnoticed.

By using "advocacy journalism," asshole reporters can make the issues on one side of a story—their side—seem strong, persuasive, and truthful, while the issues on the other side end up appearing silly, radical, or offensive—or all three.

Many of these examples of asshole journalism are easy to spot, of course. They are so blatant and crude that I sometimes suspect they are written that way deliberately. This is like the old trick of a con artist, who will let you catch on to some minor phase of the con, thereby setting you up for the larger con he has in mind. Many Americans feel smug that they can read the daily news and detect these instances of biased journalism—and they can. But what they are missing is the far more devious ploy of the assholes—censorship.

The press, of course, has always been vehemently opposed to censorship. It lobbied for and won protection from censorship in the First Amendment. It howls and screams bloody murder any time some podunk town council shuts its door in their face.

But now the media has become the very censor it has always loathed. It is deliberately and maliciously keeping certain items of relevant news from its readers and viewers, without disclaimer, apology, or warning.

Lorelei Luvanuf, a recent graduate from a famous journalism school, wrote an exposé of this very crime that appeared in *The American Spectacle* magazine as "The New Censorship of the Media." In it, she reported that her alma mater had taught its journalism students to edit the news so as to promote a list of politically correct people and issues. As they gathered all the facts for a story, they were instructed to delete anything that cast an ill light on any group on the list. This included derogatory comments, unfavorable statistics, or any facts that weakened the reputation of the key people or their causes.

The "other side," however, was not to receive the same protection. They were fair game—in fact, unfair game. If there were bad statistics or juicy rumors to report, the reporter had "an obligation" to report them—even if they had not yet been verified.

In modern journalism schools, this is called "reporting." Elsewhere, and for hundreds of years, it has been known as censorship. The fact that it is now considered a noble part of the journalistic art is a sign of how deeply the profession is directed by the Association.

Is censorship being practiced in real life journalism—and not just advocated in school? You bet it is.

One of the issues on the list is the greenhouse effect. We've heard about it for years—how the earth's temperature is slowly rising, which will eventually melt the glaciers, and produce worldwide flooding—and catastrophe. And, of course, industry is usually blamed as the "evil force" behind this phenomenon. But have you seen in print any reports on the copious scientific data and research that repudiates the basic assumptions of the greenhouse scare? It turns out there is more conclusive evidence that the earth is actually cooling slightly, instead of growing warmer! There is virtually no danger of massive flooding. Yet these studies are never printed in our newspapers and magazines or reported on TV. Why? Because the assholes do not want to lose the "shock therapy" of the greenhouse effect story.

It is relatively easy for a reporter to distort and censor the news in these ways—and get away with it. First, you find a controversy. If you want to build it up, you immediately label it a "scandal." The press, for example, labeled the Iran-Contra affair a "scandal" within 48 hours of the first news report, even though they had no evidence to support that charge—and no scandal has yet been proved in court. By contrast, the press has stoutly refused to call the Whitewater affair a scandal, even though one person has died as a probable result of it. In fact, the press has tried its hardest to make Whitewater a non-issue, and seems to be hoping it will just go away. Bias? Distortion? Or censorship?

Next, you find "experts"—usually university professors—who are willing to talk authoritatively about facts or evidence they know little about. If you choose wisely, it is a simple proposition to find someone who is willing to accuse the sun of being too hot or bright or faraway. In this way, the media gives the facts—or more likely, rumors—that they are reporting a credible spin. But the reporter chooses which way the spin will twirl—and therefore the way most readers will interpret "the news."

The ultimate degradation of the press, however, is that it has lost its integrity. Perhaps this is because the media has met the assholes and knows we are doomed. But I doubt it. Even though there are many important issues before us, from tax reform to health care reform, the hard hitting media strangely avoids them—especially on television. A topic such as health care may be brought up, but then it is treated as though it were gossip— who's the big winner, who's the big loser, and what to watch for. Reporting the news has been replaced with a game show mentality, as though Congress and the White House are the stage for a monumental game of "Dialing for Dollars."

Day in and day out, the press is far more interested in whom Senator Snort has been sleeping with—and if she feels sexually harassed—than it is with substantive issues of policy. It is far more interested in the disgruntled opinions of advocates for illegal aliens than it is with the details of legislation promoting the economy. It is far more intrigued by rumors of dissension and bickering on the White House staff than it is with true foreign policy concerns.

We would be well served if the media stopped being assholes and gave our leaders back their personal lives. It is time once again for honest discussion of the real issues confronting us—not the

107

gossip of a bunch of assholes who want to feed a controversy.

Can the media change? Of course they can. They may owe their souls to the Association, but their butts are the property of subscribers and advertisers. Write to the editor of your local paper and tell him you are on to their dirty little brown game of bias and censorship—and if it doesn't stop, you will. You will stop subscribing.

One person writing that letter won't achieve much. But 25 or 50—that will start to make a difference. And hundreds will produce a revolution.

If you can't think of anything to write, send them a sample of a modern American, just-breaking news story:

> Dateline, Your City—There appears to be no end to the brown fog that has invaded our city and settled over downtown.
>
> According to experts, the brown fog is hovering most intensely over the offices of the local daily newspaper. Other strong patches have been seen at the TV broadcast stations, city hall, and the governor's mansion.
>
> Weather experts are baffled as to the cause or source of the brown fog, but communications experts and sociologists tell us that the brown fog phenomenon has become all too familiar in major American cities in recent years.
>
> "It is the natural result of a high pressure system of pressing civic needs meeting the particulate matter of journalistic and political mudslinging, gross exaggeration, dis-

tortion, and subsequent covering up," says Harvey Cormorant, director of Sleaze and Slimebags at the prestigious Bleak House think tank.

At a news conference, the editor of the local paper, the producers of area TV news shows, and the mayor and governor all denied having any responsibility for the brown fog.

According to the man on the street, however, "It's all bullshit."

16

Song and Dance
ASSHOLISM IN ENTERTAINMENT

> Let's face it: heterosexuality just
> doesn't make an artistic statement
> anymore.
> —Choreographer Jay Gay, in an
> interview he gave just after being
> turned down for a $5,000 grant from
> the National Endowment for the
> Arts.

An old friend, Doug Gerber, invited me to lunch
one day. I had treated his wife and two kids for assholism several years before, and we had remained
friends. He was a department head at Smythe de
Clyne pharmaceuticals, and often asked me for
advice in handling some of the persistent assholes
who worked for him.

Today, though, he talked about tests he was running on some new tranquilizers and anti-depres-
sant drugs Smythe de Clyne was developing. Ordi-
narily, drug testing takes a long time and involves
elaborate cross-checks. But Doug told me that col-
laborative work they had done with the psychology

110

department of a nearby university had greatly accelerated the process.

"How is that?" I asked.

"Well, it's sheer genius. Our test group is a bunch of college and high school students. We have them watch MTV or a horror film—*Friday the 13th* or something of that genre. After 15 minutes or so of this programming, we give them the drug we are testing—intravenously, so they don't miss a beat. For the rest of the show, we monitor their emotional responses—fear, anger, or whatever. If the drug blocks out the negative response, we know we have a winner. It's that simple."

"Wait a minute," I protested. "Wouldn't you first have to identify behavioral and physiological indicators of fear, grief, or anger—and then prove that certain events reliably trigger grief, sadness, or anger? Once all of that has been done, you might have a reliable procedure for testing your drugs. But I don't remember reading any reports in the scientific literature indicating that such work has already been done."

Doug looked a bit puzzled. "Haven't I told you? The psychologists we work with at the university have been studying this for years. They have a carload of studies quantifying how much agitation is created emotionally by watching 15 minutes of MTV or a half an hour of a chainsaw murder movie. They have established that there are big shifts in heart beat, skin resistance, blood chemicals, reaction to threats, and so on.

"It's all been worked out, but they have been unable to get it published. It seems no one has the guts to be the first to state in print that rock and roll music does cause emotional and physical aberrations.

"Our scientists reviewed the data, however, and decided that it was completely sound. Violent images and sounds on TV or in a movie raise hell in people. It's like a tornado stirring up the blood pressure, adrenalin, hormones, and body chemicals. It's scary."

"That's remarkable," I said.

"Well, believe me, I don't let my kids watch that crap anymore."

We talked some more, but I had lost my appetite—an unusual event for me. Many people have long suspected that violence on TV and in the movies fosters violent behavior, but I had no idea the proof was so comprehensive.

Why wasn't the media stirring up a firestorm over this evidence? Were they unaware of it? Or had the Association intervened? Just who was censoring what?

History is filled with examples of the theater being used to promote new and complex ideas. The ancient Egyptians and Greeks used the theater to present the interaction of divine forces with human nature. Shakespeare helped establish the prestige of the British throne through his history plays. Entertainment has always been a vehicle for informing the public. It is an enjoyable way to get the message.

Charles Dickens and Victor Hugo used the novel to dramatize injustice in 19th century society. Harriet Beecher Stowe pleaded for the emancipation of black slaves in her great novel, *Uncle Tom's Cabin*. In the Roaring Twenties, Upton Sinclair wrote stories that led to reforms in the meat packing industry.

But not every writer, composer, or entertainer has the virtues or talents of a Dickens or a Sinclair. Nor do they all attempt to inspire the audience or promote a new, more humanitarian attitude on their chosen theme. In fact, fewer and fewer perform this lofty service. More often than not, our entertainments are thinly disguised excursions into hedonism, degradation, and the gutter—without any effort to lift people up to greater insights.

In the Fifties, you could be sure that the guys in the white hats would always win. Now, movie directors openly state that they hate happy endings. In recent decades, we have seen violence, drug usage, promiscuity, misogyny, misanthropy, and hostility openly celebrated and championed in the movies, on the stage, and even on television.

We have produced a generation of zombies, their brains destroyed—and controlled—by B movies, MTV, and the Home Shopping Channel. Of course, the apologists for the entertainment industry claim that they are just reflecting the interests of society. George Gottem, vice-president of a major studio, even put a shine on the issue, stating: "Our audiences know they are simply being entertained. It's all just for fun. Nobody takes these movies for real, nobody is going to be inspired by a movie to become a murderer or rapist. It's just part of life—part of our artistic statement."

Try telling that to Doug Gerber, however. He has seen proof that violence and crime do rise after exposure to the dramatization of it in a movie, TV, and popular songs. Actually, it's just common sense.

No one hijacked airplanes until D.B. Cooper did it—and the media made him a celebrity. After that, it became one of the most frustrating problems of the Seventies.

Indeed, some movies and shows are exceptional in their effort to glorify violence. One police chief in a Southern city, after viewing a popular movie that depicted the poverty and discrimination blacks must deal with, said, "It's just a goddamned training film on how to commit a robbery. That's not entertainment: it's garbage!" When this accusation made the national news, attendance for the movie shot up 20 percent.

The director of a Canadian advertising agency candidly admitted the truth of these charges in a recent interview. "We make a lot of money producing commercials that encourage people to buy the products and services of our clients. It would be hypocritical to turn around and make the claim that television images and words do not have any significant impact on the public. Of course they do—the moment they stop having an impact, we're out of a job."

Decent people already know the depth to which the entertainment industry has plunged in the last 40 years. But many of them have not investigated any further, to find out who is responsible for this rapid descent.

Who is responsible for Beavis and Butthead?

Who is responsible for theatrical works in which T-shirts are soaked in the blood of an AIDS-infected performer, then hung out to dry over the audience?

Who is responsible for rap singers who wear condoms dangling from their eyelids?

Who, for that matter, is responsible for Jane Fonda?

Is this the work of responsible, decent people?

Or is it another sign that the assholes have invaded every facet of life, and are rapidly taking over?

The assholes, of course, do not content themselves just with corrupting entertainment in obvious ways, as in the antics of Andrew Dice Clay or Sinead O'Connor—or even Madonna. Their real motive is always far more subtle, part of the secret agenda.

In the entertainment industry, the ultimate target of the Association is the hero.

In the Forties, the bad guys were thoroughly bad. The good guys were honest, hard-working, likeable fellows—the kind of guy any girl would want to marry. The police were trustworthy and the media was reliable.

Boy, how these images have changed! The bad guys are never low-lifes anymore—they are the cops, business tycoons, doctors, teachers, ministers, and lawyers. Successful people have been singled out to take the rap for almost every crime committed on either the large or small screen anymore.

And who are the heroes? They are rebels and mavericks—people who break all the rules, stir up mischief, and thumb their noses at authority. They are inevitably people with a traumatic childhood and an even less pleasant adulthood—people who ought to be in therapy, not an heroic role.

Through this shift, our old definitions of virtue, goodness, honesty, and respect for tradition become blurred. But what is even more sinister, so do our perceptions of poverty, bigotry, success, and authority.

In these artful ways, the Association has used its standing in the entertainment industry to pollute our attitudes, hopes, and expectations. All that most people want when they go to a movie or see a show on TV is to be entertained. They want to laugh and relax, or at least be challenged by a good mystery or human drama. They want to be renewed.

Instead, the American public has been given a song and dance routine. In the place of entertainment, they have been fed a tainted concoction of anti-social behavior and alienation. As a result, cynicism and pessimism have become more rooted than ever before.

It is a script that only assholes could write.

17
Flunking Out
ASSHOLISM IN EDUCATION

"Do you know your ABC's, young man," asked the teacher.
"Sure: A is for asshole, B is for bitch, C is for crapper..."
"That's quite enough!"
"Aw, rats—you didn't get to hear Q."
—*The Asshole's Primer*

Think about it: if you were a visionary asshole plotting the takeover of society, what would be one of your primary goals? The takeover of the entire educational system, from kindergarten to college. After all, if you could succeed in "dumbing down" a generation or two, society as a whole would suffer.

• The youth would be less prepared to be hired and hold jobs.

• They would be less prepared to vote intelligently.

• They would be even more susceptible to being influenced by assholes.

There are many factors responsible for the current decline in the quality of education: drugs, the rise in violence, illegitimacy, one-parent families, the breakdown in discipline, and much more. But if you look behind these factors, what will you find, manipulating and feeding them?

Assholes, of course. In specific, the Association. Let's examine the evidence.

Thirty years ago, the primary problems in school were things like gum chewing, tardiness, talking in class, and shouting in the halls. Nowadays, the list is a bit more ominous: murder, muggings, pregnancies, drug use, drug sales, drunkenness, and physical assaults on teachers.

Is the school of today prepared to cope with these problems? The answer is stated very clearly in Carole Page's autobiography, *The Classroom from Hell—My Life in the Trenches of the Teenager Wars.* In it, she described how kids would come to class drunk, stoned, or hopped up on crack. Some kids even tried to sell her nickel bags. They would pick fights in class, talk back constantly to what she was saying, and hold paper airplane contests during exams. She was physically threatened at least once a week.

Needless to say, she was not allowed to touch a student in administering discipline—by spanking, ear cuffing, or any other means. And if she sought help from the principal, she was given moral reassurance and encouragement, but no concrete assistance. Basically, she was told to endure what she could not change. Even her union steward just shrugged his shoulders when asked if there was anything the union could do to help.

One day after school had been dismissed, she walked straight into a drug deal gone bad right outside of her room. Several boys were involved, and they were going at each other with knives. Carole had the awful luck of walking right in front of a lad lunging at another. In a flash, she was at the bottom of a pile, screaming for help. She ended up suffering a broken nose, several broken ribs, and many severe lacerations. She spent three days in the hospital and several weeks at home, recuperating.

At that point, she decided she had helped the world enough. She resigned from her position at school. She ends her book, "The little bastards finally did me in." But she's not quite right. It's not the kids who did her in. It's the assholes. And even though it is likely that no member of the Association has ever set foot in your schools, you can be sure its presence has been felt there, day in and day out.

How can this be? Can the assholes really overpower decent people like this, and shove them around? Of course they can—but only if the decent people help them, by letting them have their way without challenging them. As Jack Sprat put it in his gem of a book, *The Paranoids Were Coming, But the Assholes Got Here First,* "Time after time, my investigations revealed that decent people just stood back and let assholes do their dirty work. They did nothing to stop the intimidation—in fact, they actually encouraged it, by treating the assholes as if they were decent human beings. Rudeness evoked a response of tolerance. Lying and cheating were countered with 'understanding.' Exploitation and violence were excused on the grounds that they were cries of 'pain' and 'anguish.' If the asshole belonged to a minority group, society was blamed. If it was a rich white kid, the parents were blamed.

119

"Never were the assholes exposed—or even denounced. So they kept on taking more. Parents, teachers, and administrators all held back, wanting to appear psychologically correct instead of enforcing rules and discipline. So the assholes won by default. It was more of a romp than Custer's last stand. The assholes moved in like a gang of rats invading a grocery store while authorities stood around bewildered, impotent to act."

As Edmund Burke might have said, "The only thing it takes for the assholes to triumph is for decent people to stand around and do nothing." The truth of this statement has already been demonstrated in our schools today.

Even worse, the assholes have managed to get themselves appointed to reform the mess, too. As the school system declined, responsible adults began to protest. Bond issues were no longer automatically passed. Voters started taking school board elections seriously. So the professionals had to respond.

What did they do? Instead of accepting the blame and initiating reforms themselves, they shifted responsibility.

• They said they needed more money—for equipment, teachers, and buildings.

• They said they needed metal detectors, to protect themselves and the students.

• They said tough requirements and regulations discriminated against minorities, so they relaxed them.

• They weeded out the good teachers and replaced them with complacent ones who would not rock the boat.

Naturally, no real progress occurred; any genuine effort to reform was immediately stomped on by an asshole. The assholes have managed to tie up the educational establishment in a morass of sub-mediocre performance. A gridlock among administrators, the teachers' union, the school boards, and public officials is strangling education in almost every major city in the country—and most suburban and rural schools, too.

This kind of dissension is the asshole's playground—a perfect stage for a brown takeover. In her book, *Assholes Are Contagious,* Alice Goober presents convincing evidence that one of the great talents of assholes is the ability to promote dissension until all cooperation and progress grinds to a halt.

"I used to watch some of the assholes where I worked plot how they were going to 'get the boss.' Then, whenever a problem came up—usually because they screwed up—the accusations would begin to fly. The work load was too great. Assignments were unfair. Equipment was breaking down. Other departments were slowing us down. The net result was that productivity was low and we were constantly extending deadlines. In one year, they managed to sabotage three different bosses."

(Mrs. Goober followed this book with the story of her family life, entitled *My Five Assholes.* The title referred to her husband, whom she divorced, and her four children, whom she couldn't.)

I suspected that Goober's insights into the work place also applied to our schools, so I did a little investigating of my own. I asked one of the leaders of the ANAL workshops in Chicago, Denise, to check out a few theories for me. Denise was a teacher's assistant at one of the city's schools. I suggested that she speak to some union people, members of the PTA, some teachers, and some local activists, and ask them—off the record—to comment on what changes needed to be made to repair our educational system.

I hit pay dirt. A month later, Denise sent me a report of her interviews. As expected, the teachers blamed the administration. The administration blamed the teachers' union—and the community, for not giving them enough money. The school board blamed the government for strangling them with too many rules and restrictions.

I had expected all of this; the gold mine was tapped when she talked to the local activists. Some of them were proud of how they had kept the school board from implementing new performance standards—"We blackmailed the bastards into granting our demands. If the teachers don't have to perform up to standards, my kids sure as hell won't, either."

But that was nothing compared to the antics of Louella, whom Denise coaxed into talking after buying her several drinks. Louella was known as the queen of multiculturalism in her community. She began by bragging how she had held up the purchase of new school texts for three years because she did not like the way the books described blacks, Eskimos, Arabs, or native Americans. A few drinks later, she admitted she didn't give a damn about anyone but the blacks—she just wanted to punish the school board for snubbing her in previous years.

She then went on to explain to Denise that she had recruited other organizations to help her harass the school board. Two that she mentioned were TAKE (Teachers After Kinder Economics) and GRAB (Generous Rewards and Bonuses). She candidly admitted she couldn't stand "the greedy sonsofbitches" that run these organizations, but she had no qualms about using them for her own purposes.

"When the administration gets too snotty, " she continued, "I remind them that they expel too many blacks. I charge them with discrimination. When there are too many fights in class, I charge them with negligence. And when kids flunk out, I charge the school with incompetence. I have them coming and going. They can't do a thing without kissing my big fat ass, honey—because they know I can get people from TAKE and GRAB, the city council, and even the EEOC to attack them.

"I've tied them up in knots. I got 'em both ways, and there is no way in hell they can fix the mess I created for them!"

Louella, obviously, is a mega-asshole, and proud to be one. She claims to be concerned about education, but she is actually the one stirring up division and distrust. The community could take one giant step forward in improving the educational scene just by giving Louella a police escort to the edge of town. It would not be politically correct, but it would at least be effective. It would let decent citizens take over control of their schools again.

It is not money, or better text books, or computers that will make our education better. The most important step is the very first one:

Kick out the assholes.

123

18
Bible Banging
For Fun and Profit
ASSHOLISM IN RELIGION

> Some say that assholes invented
> religion, but that's not true. They're
> just the ones who kicked out God.
> —from *Dr. Crement's Pocket Guide
> To Surviving Assholes*

By now, most decent people are quite aware of
the monstrous hyprocrisy and malice of fundamentalists. Those who are not should read Jennifer Jelly's enlightening account, *Poison in the Pul-
pit.* You will never view the clergy—or assholes—
the same again.

Jennifer writes from an insider's perspective;
she had been the aide to Diane Swinehart, a popular TV evangelist, for several years. But then they
had a falling out—Diane started treating Jennifer
like an asshole—so Jennifer split. The book became a bestselling bombshell when it was published.

"We would do everything we could," Jennifer writes, "to stir up a sense of doom and fear in the people attending our meetings. We would tell them the devil was waiting to take them away and torture them for their sins. We would remind them of the everlasting fires in hell. They must fear God, and if they did not obey the word of God—i.e., whatever we told them—God would wax mighty in His wrath and send down a horrible affliction as punishment. By halfway through the service, they feared both God and the devil. We were the only ones they could trust. We had them both coming and going.

"Of course, that was just the set up. To keep them enslaved to us, we had to promise them something more than just protection from supernatural terror. The bait that hooked them every time was money and healing. We promised that for every $10 they gave us, for the work of the Lord, God would return to them $1,000. We just made those figures up, of course, but they appealed to an awful lot of greedy sinners.

"The other scam, healing, was even easier. We got some cranky little old ladies up at the altar and got them so high on excitement that they forgot about their mostly imaginary aches and pains for a while. We had them dancing in the aisles. It worked like a charm—the money just kept rolling in. It was like stealing candy from a baby."

These schemes and ploys are so transparent that you have to be half an asshole yourself to get suckered into them in the first place. I have little sympathy for the people who get ripped off by evangelists. They aren't Christians any more than the people leading the services are.

I mention fundamentalism because it reveals the unadulterated influence of assholism in religion today. I truly think that fundamentalism needs to be declassified as a religion and reclassified as assholism. That's right—they should lose their tax free status and their various immunities from prosecution. It's time they were forced into honest work.

Because my views on the assholism of fundamentalism are well known, I was surprised last year when I was invited by one of the lesser known evangelists to give a lecture at a seminar on "social justice and family values" at a nearby Christian college. My host said he wanted to bury the hatchet and educate his colleagues as to how they are perceived by others.

What I didn't know was that he wanted to bury the hatchet in my scalp. His invitation was just a trap to get me in a setting where they could attack me.

I had just defined assholism when the assault began.

"Aren't you just doing the devil's work?" one shouted.

"Get thee behind me, Satan!" cried another.

I quieted them down a little by thanking them for demonstrating the rudeness and intimidation that are the primary characteristics of assholes, thereby making my task easier. But the attack was not over; they just shifted gears.

"Aren't you undermining the faith of the innocent by encouraging them to think for themselves?" asked one Southern gentleman. "How can they ever find God by thinking for themselves?"

"I don't think God is worried about that at all," I quipped. "God gave us a mind so that we could learn to think. If we have the freedom to think, sooner or later our minds will reveal God."

They all shuddered at that thought. But the smooth gentleman from the South—slick is probably the better word—was not through. "In that case, you should have no problem leaving us alone to pursue our chosen calling. And yet you accuse us of being shams. You say our healing ministry is a fraud. Aren't you being a hypocrite?"

"Not at all," I replied. "I am just being true to my Hippocratic oath. As a physician, I try to heal, not harm. To heal, I must respect each patient's potential for becoming a decent human being. I must also protect him from any forces which might undermine that healing.

"Most of you undermine true healing, instead of promoting it. As a doctor, I know it. And you know it, too. You just won't admit it in public."

I might as well have waved a squirrel at a pack of nasty dogs. The ministers erupted into a frenzy of damnation and curses such as I have never heard before. I wanted to tell the sons of bitches that they were the ones doing the devil's work, not me, and that the damnation and blight would fall on their heads, not mine. But since Captain Kirk was not overhead in the starship Enterprise, waiting with Scotty to beam me up, I refrained from making any more incendiary remarks. I simply walked out and left the assholes as I had found them.

In my opinion, every one of them would deserve to be in the Asshole hall of fame, if there were one. Let's face it: fundamentalism is just bad religion—

religion that has been corrupted by embracing too many assholes.

But bad religion is not limited just to fundamentalism. It can be found in any denomination.

One of the most common signs of bad religion is the corrupt idea that we can serve God by hating evil. For centuries, the church taught us to hate the devil. Most of us have outgrown that pagan piety, but we are still influenced and guided by the idea behind it—that it is desirable to hate evil.

Yet any kind of hate is destructive and anti-spiritual. It alienates us from God and keeps us obsessed with what makes us miserable. So by teaching us to hate evil, the assholes are still generating bad religion.

Religion has been a target of the Association for so long that the damage is incalculable. History records that Machiavelli was the first philosopher to promote the idea that the end justifies the means. This is not strictly true. The church had been guided by this formula for centuries before Machiavelli conceived of *The Prince.*

They have used this concept as a license to start wars, to excommunicate whole nations, to confiscate property, and to kill off the joy and self-respect of untold millions, all in the name of doing God's will. And this neat principle of exploitation is still the most common clerical justification for bending rules and excusing criminal behavior.

Another sure sign of religion gone bad is the heavy emphasis on guilt. The goal of religion should be to encourage us to celebrate the splendors and beauties of God's life. Instead, the assholes have turned this principle topsy-turvy, by trying to make us feel guilty about all the problems of the world—almost none of which we caused.

Nothing is more devastating than persistent guilt. It disables our ability to redeem ourself by creating a state of self-rejection—as opposed to growth. We begin to fear retribution, thereby weakening our desire to try again, until we get it right. Worst of all, guilt creates the illusion that God has already judged us and found us unworthy—unworthy of further assistance. By default, the only option left to us appears to be to endure the hardships of life with a grinding, continuous sense of failure.

As a psychiatrist, I find that guilt is often the most corrosive factor preventing healing. The dark side of religion has corrupted mass consciousness into believing that guilt is an appropriate response to our failings.

How much of a problem is it? There is enough guilt in the world today to keep therapists busy helping people work it out for eons to come. Who do we have to thank for it? The assholes who founded the dark side of religion and exploited it.

Some members of the church have recognized the problems bad religion has created in society. But in all too many cases, they have then gone too far in the other direction to correct these problems. As a result, there are churches today that have a very tepid agenda. Their creed is voiced but not followed. Their doctrines are flabby and mostly unrelated to daily life. And it is hard to discern the purpose they serve, beyond self-congratulatory praise for being so "spiritual."

This leads to some pretty shaky theology, as

demonstrated by the Rev. Woody Feelgoode, pastor of the "New, New, and Even Newer Age of God Church." In a recent sermon, Woody told his congregation, "All of us are spiritual already—we just do not know it yet."

This is a good example of how the permissiveness of our modern generation—another gift from the assholes—has filtered into the church and produced bad religion of a different hue and stripe.

In Woody's scheme of things, the quality of your character and life seem unimportant, just as long as you believe that you are God's "wonderful" creation. In fact, you were created so perfectly that almost no effort is necessary to achieve full attunement with God. Cats and dogs probably qualify for baptism in his church.

In fact, one long-time member of Woody's church once commented to me that his stupefying sermons sometimes made her suspect that religion might possibly cause brain damage.

Religion was never meant to become the playground of eggheaded theologians, arguing over the virgin birth. Nor was it meant to become just another social club where the singing is good and the coffee is free.

The greatest evidence of the almost total control of religion by the assholes is a simple one. Just walk into any church or synagogue and ask yourself, "Does God live here? Or has He moved out in disgust years ago, tired of being misrepresented by the bigots, the Bible-bangers, and the do-gooder bleeding hearts? Who would move in?"

The only ones with the temerity to do so would be the assholes.

Whenever I attack bad religion in this way, people often wonder if I am an atheist. I am not. I have found real help in working with higher power, and I encourage my patients to look for and find it, too. This need for God is reinforced at ANAL workshops, too.

But I have always believed that religion is supposed to serve God. When the image of God is twisted and distorted in ways that serve only the church and the clergy, I draw the line.

I believe in God, not religious crap.

As Molly, one of our ANAL leaders said recently, "There is more God in the basement of churches where our workshops are held than in the sanctuary upstairs." She then went on to tell me that they invited the minister to attend some of their meetings, but she finally had to ask the minister to leave. "He was a real downer on the group. All he could talk about was despair and sin. He freaked out some people so badly they never came back. We had to ask him to stay away. As a result, we had to move to the Baptist church across town, but at least we could get back to our agenda."

It is time that we see that the agenda of the modern church is controlled by the Association. Here and there a few intelligent, God-centered clergy are working, as voices crying in the wilderness. But these few brave souls are not enough to hold back the brown tide.

The tide, unfortunately, is rising. Let us all pray for deliverance.

19
Assholes at Work
ASSHOLISM IN BUSINESS

> "Here's an example of good business.
> I will sell you this bottle of perfume,
> which I bought for a buck, for $20."
> "Isn't that stealing?" asked Alice.
> "Good heavens, no," said the Walrus.
> "You are getting the goods you've
> paid for. It's called mark-up."
> "It seems like stealing to me," insisted
> Alice.
> "Obviously," the Walrus sniffed,
> "you've never heard of overhead,
> taxes, and profit."
> "You are right," said Alice. "But I
> have heard of whistle-blowing. Have
> you?"
> —*Malice in Wonderland*

Anyone who doubts that there are assholes in business should go out and buy a used car. Those who doubt that there is a *conspiracy* of assholes in business need look no further than the tobacco industry.

Tobacco is probably the most widely-used addic-

132

tive substance in the world. There may very well be more people addicted to nicotine than to alcohol and all other drugs put together. The total cost of this addiction is enormous—sick leave, health care costs, and death benefits.

And yet, the tobacco industry swears that tobacco is not addictive. So far, it has successfully avoided paying out damages on any lawsuit filed on behalf of victims of lung cancer or emphysema, who claim that cigarets did them in.

They have also managed to dodge legislation in Congress that might put them out of business—or restrict their very generous subsidies severely.

Is this just a coincidence? Or is the tobacco industry under the control of assholes?

It would be incorrect to say that all business is under the thumb of the Association. But the evidence strongly suggests that certain facets of it may well be:

• Advertising, for example, is tailor made for assholes—a perfect forum for the lying, cheating, and bullshit that characterises assholism. And when advertising becomes the primary cost in a product's pricing—as in soft drinks, cosmetics, and other goods—is this just the marketplace at work? Or is it the work of assholes?

• When businesses charge customers a minimum of $200 for a service call—even if only five minutes of work is required—is this free enterprise? Or is it assholism?

• When a company charges $65 for a refill of a lubricant that is available in any drugstore for less than $2, is this a fair business practice—or is it the modern day equivalent of highway robbery?

• When business people complain about excessive governmental rules and restrictions on Monday and then demand tariff protection from foreign imports on Tuesday, is this the American way? Or is it another sign of assholes at work?

• When banks charge customers $24 or more to process a bounced check, even though the actual costs incurred amount to less than $2, and then complain about how much it inconveniences them, are they being reasonable and honest? Or are they just covering up their own scandalous behavior with an outrageous brown smokescreen?

There is both good news and bad news about assholism in the business world. The bad news is that the Super Browns have made substantial inroads into the business hierarchy. The good news is that the progress they have made in this regard is not nearly as great as in government, religion, and the media.

The lure of business to the asshole is the great wealth that can be accumulated through a successful business career. The hard work and competence that is required to attain this wealth is not very appealing to most assholes, however, who are by nature lazy. Those assholes who are dominated by sloth go into government or the ministry, where the pickings are easier. After all, all an asshole has to do in order to become a bureaucratic tyrant is pass a simple civil service test—a test that was undoubtedly written by other assholes. All a Bible-banging asshole has to do is be "called by God"—a simple act of the imagination—and start hustling donations to support his "ministry."

The assholes who are left to go into business are

those who are actually capable of hard work and some sacrifice. In all likelihood, they will need to cheat their way to a good education before they can cheat their way to the top levels of their chosen industry.

For this reason, those assholes who do survive the ardors of business life usually end up being the sharpest, most conniving assholes of all. They know what it means to climb up on the backs of the fallen, and they have long since killed any sense of remorse or conscience that might have indicated that they still nurtured a shred of decency.

In other words, the assholes that make it big in business are prime material for the Association. In fact, they probably have received help somewhere along the line from the Super Browns.

The Super Browns are not just interested in the executive suite, however. They have also been careful to nurture strong candidates in the unions—and there are plenty of them.

The unions, after all, have become the most capitalistic of everyone in capitalism.

Under the normal course of evolution, the unions and management would have come together years ago and buried the hatchet. It should be clear to anyone but an idiot that both the unions and management have identical goals. The only quarrel is who gets how much of the profits—an issue that even thieves generally resolve. The fact that the unions and management remain miles apart, and view each other as antagonists to the death, is proof that the Association is hard at work in the business world, keeping this conflict from the last century alive and thriving artificially.

How can one tell an asshole business person from a decent business person? Look at the services and goods they provide. If it is a solid product sold at a reasonable price, you can probably be sure that it is not being offered by an asshole.

On the other hand, if it is shoddy merchandise— or an unneeded service—offered at far more than it is worth, you can be sure an asshole is involved somewhere.

If you take your car in for routine servicing, and it performs more poorly after $700 worth of repairs than it did before, you have been taken by an asshole.

If you buy a diamond ring at 50 percent off, and are then told by an appraiser that it is worth only one-twentieth of what you paid, you have been taught an expensive lesson by an asshole.

If you order a dozen computer terminals from a company, only to find out that you will have to spend an extra $5,000 getting new electrical service or they cannot be installed, you have just been screwed by an asshole.

Often, business assholes will be in cahoots with government assholes. How else can you explain the following scenario? Fred puts his house on the market and sells it for a reasonable price. Just prior to the closing, he finds out that the year before the county had adopted new regulations, and he must spend $4,000 to upgrade his sewage system—or the house cannot be sold. The current sewage system is good enough for him, but not good enough for anyone else. Fred cannot remember voting on this change, and for good reason. It wasn't voted on. It was passed by the county commissioners, right after those massive campaign contributions came in from the local plumbers and backhoe operators.

The greatest achievement for a business asshole is when he can persuade his friends in government (other members of the Association) to mandate that only the product that he makes can be used in schools, hospitals, or other major installations. There is nothing like a legal monopoly to milk the cow dry.

In his landmark book, *How To Swim With the Barracudas and Float with the Turds,* Harry "Sharky" Finn lists four new laws of assholism in the marketplace.

"The old rule used to be, 'Never give a sucker an even break.' This is too easy on the sucker. So the old rule has been replaced by four new laws:

"The first law of assholism: Always cheat, if you think you can get away with it. If you don't cheat when you have the opportunity, you can be sure some other asshole will, and knock you to the wayside.

"In fact, cheating needs to be extended into new areas. Information is one of those new areas—it has become the equivalent of money and power. So make sure that important letters and memos never reach other people in your department.

"If you can, substitute false or misleading instructions. Send the guy at the next desk off on some wild goose chase that will make him look like an idiot.

"The second rule of assholism: Bullshit, bullshit, and more bullshit. If information is money and power, then bullshit is the ammunition you need to attack your competition, to give reports, and to persuade customers to buy, buy, buy. Get good at it.

"The third law of assholism: Silence is golden—especially when you are accused of malfeasance. Since the charge is probably true, you do not want to give it any credence, even by denying it.

"The fourth law of assholism: learn to delegate wisely. If it is blame, pass it along—blame it on someone else. If it is praise or a reward, grab it all for yourself."

Finn's work is aimed at helping the petty asshole climb out of his smallmindedness. The atmosphere is far more rarefied in the world of Donald Crump, who writes about it in his bestseller, *The Art of the Steal.* Commenting on the art of high finance, he writes:

"After you toss out figures over a half-billion dollars, peoples' eyes just glaze over. You can say most anything after that. They get so excited that they just go gaga. Pretty soon, they are signing the contracts—even without reading them!"

Crump goes on to report that he went from working at McDonald's at age sixteen to being a multibillionaire in just twenty years. He attributed most of his success to a combination of unusual accounting practices and extremely unusual property appraisals, blended with "under the table" incentives for selected banking executives. But the keystone to the Crump approach is hype—the brown fog of bullshit.

"Before I walk into a boardroom, I have made the people I am meeting with so in awe of me that they believe I can walk on water, read minds, and blow gold coins out of my nose! They are so intimidated that, to them, I become like the Pope chewing out a

138

nun. I'm half way home to getting my way even before we begin."

There is no question that there are plenty of assholes in business, including any number of Super Browns. But the Association is still largely operating from the fringes. The very nature of business demands at least a minimal level of productivity, and that is not in the nature of assholes. Sooner or later, even the greediest and most devious of these predators overextends himself and self-destructs.

Is it possible that capitalism is the Achilles' heel of the mega-asshole?

20
Art With a Capital "F"
ASSHOLISM IN THE ARTS

A cross-eyed old painter named Jeff
Was color-blind, palsied, and deaf;
    When he asked to be touted
    The critics all shouted,
"This is art, with a capital F!"
—old limerick

In days gone by, whenever I needed an afternoon of psychological renewal, I would drive down to our local art museum and immerse myself in the works of the great masters. I called it "visiting Rembrandt."

One of the great shocks of my life came after the museum acquired a new director. I arrived for one of my occasional visits, only to find Rembrandt and his friends locked away in "storage." In their place, the walls were filled with what can only charitably be called "art." They were canvases filled with ugliness, chaos, and banality. I began to cry, and then in desperation, ran from room to room, looking for my former loves. They had all been removed. I left the museum, silently screaming.

I couldn't believe it. This shrine to beauty, this

wonderful, magical place where I had always before found peace, comfort, and reinvigoration, had become a chamber of horrors.

When I got back to the office, I called the chairman of the Friends of the Museum.

"What is going on at the gallery?" I asked.

"What do you mean?" he replied.

"That crap on the wall—did anyone ask for it?"

"No one asked for it," was the answer. "It's the work of the new director. He felt the gallery was behind the times. It's our new emphasis on modern art."

"Well, it's awful," I said. "You have let him ruin a place of beauty."

"The critics love it," the chairman replied.

"Well, let me ask you one thing. Are any of the critics members of the museum? Do you get any large checks from critics, as you have from me?"

"No," came the meek response.

"Well, until you and the director learn to ask me what I like in art, try getting donations from the critics!" I hung up and canceled all future gifts.

The art world is not a high priority to the Association, because not that many people actually pay attention to it anymore. But the creative world still does play a significant, behind the scenes role of influencing the thinking and aspirations of the masses. So the art world does figure into the plans and goals of the Super Browns.

In fact, there may well be more assholes in the arts today than decent people. If you look at many canvases of what is called "modern art," you will quickly be convinced that only assholes could create them.

141

As Spike Sezso, columnist for the *Pittsburgh Pit,* wrote: "Most of the modern crap is worse than the graffiti that is sprayed on building walls. I'd rather look at a pile of dogshit than most of this art. At least I would know what I'm looking at—and why. And the message would be honest."

Art critics, of course, dismiss Sezso as uninformed and ill-advised. They claim that art has simply moved on to new levels of sophistication where the message is more subtle and important than the image or form.

To these people, a pile of garbage on the museum floor is no longer just garbage; it is a political statement condemning the nature of society. A shower curtain hanging over a bathtub in a gallery is not just an unimaginative, utilitarian form; it is a commentary on boundaries, privacy, and the fact that we all stand naked at times. A large brown canvas with one vertical black stripe is said to depict the struggle of Afro-Americans in the literal and figurative dirt of America.

Just who decided that art should depict fear, violence, poverty, and pessimism—instead of hope, beauty, compassion, and optimism? It wasn't me— and I bet it wasn't you. It was those assholes.

Just who decided that crudeness was a valid art form? Who decided that a pile of trash in the middle of the floor was actually a piece of art—and not just something the janitor needs to toss? It wasn't me— and again I would bet it wasn't you. It was the assholes.

The fact that you won't find any of this junk in commercial galleries is proof of the asshole conspiracy. No one wants to buy it and hang it in their living rooms; it can only be displayed at public galleries, where we can all suffer together.

The same pattern can be observed in modern dance, in the theater, and in literature. The arts have been hijacked by a bunch of screwball assholes who want to thrust their bile and rage down our throats. It seems as if the world of arts has become nothing but a platform for assholes to criticize society, a stage on which they can celebrate pessimism and the dark side of human nature.

A recent article in the *American Review* reports on how pervasively this attitude of doom has penetrated our intellectual life. In the article, "A New Enthusiasm for Pessimism," the author chronicles how fiction writing is being taught in the university.

"Courses in creativity have been radicalized by just a handful of anti-social malcontents. Great contempt—as well as failing grades—is reserved for those students who dare to write about mainstream America—or even worse, choose to end on an upbeat note. A relentless pressure is placed on the students to emphasize political grievances and social problems—in the name of 'realism,' of course.

"The hero of modern American college writing is always a victim. The villain is always society."

Do parents know what they are getting when they pay $20,000 a year in tuitions, so that their sons and daughters can get an education? Don't they deserve something a little bit better than exposing their children to assholes?

A very popular painter in limited circles is Cicely Sickum, who has been hailed as a premier feminist artist. She specializes in large paintings of victims of rape—and portraits of naked men with their testicles cut off or their penises being tortured. Her most famous canvas, titled "Homage to Lorena," shows a male penis being cut off with scissors.

"All art is a message," Ms. Sickum claims, "and the message is that we are sick! Society is sick. Men are sick. And women are sick and tired of being abused. My art merely shows what is real—what is happening all the time. I expect those who see my art to be just as full of rage as I am about all the injustice in the world."

But is the world that sick? Didn't Rembrandt and da Vinci live at times when men beat their wives and wives beat their husbands, during times of war and plague and all kinds of awful stuff? Are their paintings filled with grief and despair? Of course not. Are they any less inspired for that reason? Of course not. Are they any less real? Only an asshole would ever think so.

Real art has always been a celebration of the creative vision and inner beauty the artist sees. Art can inspire us to appreciate the subtle, to sense the relationships we have with others, nature, and even divine life. Real art leads us on a discovery of what life really means—not just an awareness of what is wrong.

Modern art—and dance, literature, and the theater—is obsessed with the dark side of life for only one reason. The artists of today have been seduced by the Association.

The next time you go to a museum and are confronted with a pile of trash that claims to be art, sweep it up and give it a proper burial. Just make sure no one is looking.

21
Invasion of the Assholes
ASSHOLISM IN PSYCHOLOGY

> "Mirror, mirror, on the wall,
> Whose the greatest victim of them
> all?"
> "I am," the mirror whined. "You've
> looked at me so often that I'm
> cracked."
> —from *Mom and Pop Psychology, a
> Guide For Parents Who Are Victims*

"We are all victims," the gurus of the latest craze in pop psychology pronounce.

"Bullshit," intelligent people respond. "No one is a victim, except of his or her own propaganda. You are just unrecovered assholes."

Fortunately, pop psychology does not embrace the full scope of modern psychology, just the fringes of it. But the intensity with which the victim rage has spread is a sobering indication of how much of modern psychology is controlled by assholes.

Orginally, psychology was aimed at helping relieve human suffering, especially in the emotional and mental realms. People sometimes work themselves into some pretty bizarre distortions of maturity, and psychology arose to help them reconstruct a decent, healthy life.

But what began as the study and treatment of disorders of the human psyche has evolved into something quite different. Somewhere, a branch of modern psychology took a wrong turn. That's when the assholes slipped in.

You can be sure that assholes are on the scene when screaming and infantile behavior ceases to be signs of neurosis and magically becomes a form of therapy.

You can be sure that assholes have become entrenched when treatment becomes nothing but a sympathetic validation of a client's suffering, instead of directing him or her toward a resolution of the problem.

You can likewise be sure that assholes are at work when "supporting the patient" comes to mean helping clients find better rationalizations for their whining and blaming.

It's almost as if modern psychology has become a way of teaching people how to become better assholes! That wasn't what Freud devoted his life to. But it's what's happening.

I am a psychiatrist, and I don't remember ever being polled and asked if I thought psychology ought to change its course in these ways. But it has occurred, anyway. Why is that?

The assholes invaded psychology—and were accepted without challenge.

Under the assholes, psychology has stopped encouraging people to become more mature. It has devoted itself to teaching people how to rediscover their anger, expand their selfishness, and bully others into getting what they want. It even sounds like a short course in assholism, doesn't it?

Of course, the assholes do not advertise their therapies in quite this way. Being assholes, they know how to use their little brown tricks to confuse unsuspecting people.

• Clients are not encouraged to bully others— just be assertive and stand up for their rights!

• Patients are never told to be selfish—just "self-nurturing."

• No one is ever told to be angry, either—but they are told they must "rediscover" their anger and learn to use it for change.

When did selfishness, hostility, and defensiveness stop being signs of blatant immaturity and become part of "the search for wholeness"?

Right about the time the assholes took over.

Naturally, I had seen the signs of incipient assholism in psychology for many years. But I only began to suspect that psychology was an important target of the Association when I read Ernest Lemmingway's great book, *Assholes Also Rise,* in which he explains how troublemaking assholes bully, cheat, exhaust, or just drive you crazy, until they gain control. He writes:

"Even average assholes have worked out successful methods of manipulating others to get what they want. Yet, they are so stupid and self-absorbed that they rarely know what they *do* want. And so they claim they are weak and need your help. Or they claim they have been neglected, and need your indulgence. Or they claim special rights and privileges, and demand your cooperation. And if none of

147

these ploys works, they will just drive you nuts with fussing and nagging and whining and yelling— until you are willing to do anything to get a few moments of peace.

"Clearly, assholes expect you to fix their problems for them—by granting all their wishes and accepting them the way they are. If any changes must be made, you are expected to make them all. They are not going to be happy until you have given into all their selfish demands—a vague day in the future which will never arrive.

"Assholes win as you give in. By default, they rise and you fall!"

From Lemmingway's description, it should be obvious that the Association has been successful in snaring the allegiance of a large number of counselors and teachers of psychology. Indeed, this invasion of the field of psychology may be the most devastating thrust of the Super Browns to date. This is because psychology is the very institution which should be in the vanguard, teaching us how to spot assholes. Now that it has fallen to the assholes themselves, who is left to lead the way?

The *coup de grâce* of the Association's invasion of psychology is surely the publication and tremendous popularity of the recent bestseller, *How To Win the Victim Game.* In it, pop psychologist Dorothy Ufoz presents a step-by-step program for becoming a happy and satisfied victim. She claims to have helped hundreds of thousands of pathetic people learn to use their disabilities to make their life work better. She writes, "Once you understand that a minor illness or complaint can be your ticket to a life of comfort, protection, and support by your family—

and society, too—the game of life becomes much easier."

Unfortunately, our view of maturity and values has become so debased that many decent people have a hard time resisting these sociopathic rationalizations.

This is why the asshole invasion of the field of psychology is so damaging to us all. Decent people have no trouble seeing the foolishness of the more bizarre distortions of psychology. If someone came to you and promised to greatly improve your self-esteem by teaching you a new fad—bungee jumping without the cord—would you believe him? Of course not! But would you accept a *gradual* shift in our social attitudes, and begin to believe that nearly everyone is a victim of society—and the truly disadvantaged victims can only be helped if we give them special treatment, new incentives, and a free pass? The truth is, you probably already have.

In one brilliant move, the Association has succeeded in turning our society upside down. No longer are the healthy, productive, sensible people able to set the tone for society and establish its values. We have turned over these functions to the sickest, most immature, and most selfish people.

Of course, by their definition, they are not even sick anymore—we are. Society is.

Any effort to point out the truth will draw the assholes from the woodwork, shouting, "You are just blaming the victim." I have had that accusation yelled at me at many of my lectures throughout the country. I have even been hit by people throwing my books at me. (I hope they paid for them first.)

I just remind them that even assholes can grow

up and become decent human beings—but only assholes would ever think of making a career out of being a victim. I tell them they are fat—bloated with self-created rage—and need to go on a diet in which they stop whining and fussing and learn to become a mature person. But they don't want to listen to reason; they just want to whine and complain. They have bought in completely to the asshole view of life.

I have seen the tragedies that have resulted from the asshole invasion of psychology. It is not a pretty picture. As a psychiatrist, I despair to see my chosen profession trashed in this way. But it is happening, so we must not pretend it is not. We need to deal with this invasion firmly and squarely.

Yes, we must do what psychologists have long resisted doing. It will be a strain, especially for everyone in California. But there is no alternative. If we are to take our profession back, we must *grow up*. We must demonstrate what it means to be and act as a mature, decent adult.

This is guaranteed to send the assholes running!

Part Five:
The Need
for a Social Enema

22

Dr. Crement's Prescription

> Life doesn't begin until the cheating stops.
> —*Dr. Crement's Pocket Guide To Surviving Assholism*

Can the tide of assholism in society be stopped? Can we return to our usual standards of decency and goodwill?

Of course we can—if we have the will to do so. It will not be easy, because the momentum amassed by the Association is great. The danger of a total takeover by the assholes is very real. But decent people still outnumber the assholes by a large margin. Unless we stand back and do nothing at all, we should be able to purge society of these asshole traits and influences.

This is just what society needs, in fact—a massive enema that will cleanse every institution of the deadening presence of the Super Browns. We have to clean the assholes out, and give society a chance to start afresh again—with clearer values, stronger principles, and a renewed enthusiasm. We need to unite and take back the high position we used to have in government, education, and religion.

To win against assholes, you have to be able to think like one. As we have seen, assholes constantly pursue what they believe to be money, power, and control. But they always want more! More money, more power, more attention, more pleasure. If they think you have it, they want it.

Being self-absorbed and lazy, however, they assume that they have to cheat in order to get it. Herein lies a blind spot, an Achilles' heel that we can take aim at. They are convinced that only people who scheme and cheat ever win at anything. We must take their game away from them, by proving that this is not true.

First, we must remind them that there is a great risk in cheating and scheming. Eventually, you get caught. And when you do, everything you have schemed for tends to fall apart. You may be sent to prison. You will probably lose your job, perhaps your family. The friends you have conned will abandon you. It is not pleasant being a failed asshole.

Secondly, and much more importantly, we must show them dramatically that people who play their games with honesty and decency do better than assholes do—and without having to worry about being caught in illegal or immoral acts.

It is true that assholes sometimes make a lot of money, but so do decent human beings. And they get to enjoy their wealth their whole life—not just until they are thrown in jail.

It is true that propaganda sometimes sways the opinions of millions of people. But the truth is even more appealing, and always wins out in the end.

It is true that rationalizations and excuses can cover up many misdeeds. But the cover up can only be sustained for awhile, and then it will blow up in the asshole's face. Sincere, constructive efforts need no cover ups.

It is true that society has problems, but no one needs to be a victim of either society or its problems. These problems give decent human beings the opportunity to improve themselves, by hurdling over them.

The idea is to hit the assholes where they live, to shake their unfounded confidence and make them start to question their basic assumptions. There are four stages to this process.

1. Good people must become alert to the danger of allowing society to be heavily influenced by assholes.

2. These people must organize to take back the high ground and promote the values and lifestyle of decency.

To some degree, the machinery for achieving the first two steps has already been implemented, through the appearance of my books, the writings of others, and classes and lectures we have held.

3. We must then confront and neutralize the steady stream of propaganda assholes issue. We must expose their lies, their distortion of facts, their misleading use of statistics, their obsession with misery, and their tendency to shirk responsibility.

When Gloria Stoneham tells us that she must assume that all men are potential rapists until they prove themselves safe to women, we must fight back by pointing out the vicious sexual tone of this accusation. We must turn the tables, asking if it would then be okay for men to assume that all women are bitches until they prove otherwise? Or, if a woman without a man is like a fish without a bicycle, then isn't it just as true that a man without a woman is like an elephant without an accordion? Sexism is not just a one-way street. And the victims of sexism are not just women.

This opens up a whole new vein of dialogue. Are we to construe Ms. Stoneham's comments as indicating that a black without a white is like a xylophone without a faucet? Or that all blacks are potential muggers until they can prove themselves honest? It's all nonsense, and Ms. Stoneham knows it. But she won't change her monotonous tone until we rub her nose in her own bullshit.

Can we assume that men have the right to lie and cheat because a few women—like Ms. Stoneham herself—do so? Bigotry is an equal opportunity offender, and Ms. Stoneham is just as corrupt, even more so, than the people she points her guilty finger at.

When Malcolm Y tells us that all white people are oppressors and should be regarded, collectively, as the devil, decent people of all races need to answer with the truth. The truth is that both Indians and other blacks owned slaves as well as whites in the South prior to the Emancipation; it is a matter of historical record. Exploitation is not a function of the color of a person's skin; it is a function of assholism. So is the willful distortion of the truth.

If we are to stop assholism in its tracks, we must stop letting demagogues mug the truth on a daily basis. When they spout forth their message of hate and bigotry, good people must stand up and label it for what it is:

Bullshit.

When Dan Blather or Michael Kinsin tells us that the only way to solve our social problems is to increase the size and power of government, we need to fight back. We must remind them that three decades and billions of dollars invested in "their solutions" have failed to produce results—and may have actually made things worse.

Education is a case in point. Ever since Jimmy Carter created a Department of Education—which meant massive federal funds could be spent on schooling—the test scores of our students have steadily declined. Is this a good return on our investment? And the drop is most dramatic among the poor and disadvantaged. Decent people must not let the assholes get away with this kind of nonsense. The money spent on lowering these test scores could be better spent in our own pockets!

It is time to hold the assholes accountable, and that is what Step 3 is all about. We have to stop letting them hoodwink us with their smiles and promises and disastrous performances. Compassion, after all, comes in many shapes and sizes. Some brands work, and some just make things worse. Asshole compassion is guaranteed to make life worse!

Of course, if we begin to hold the assholes accountable, they will cry out for the need for truth squads to protect them against our "vicious smears." This will actually be a good sign—an indication that we have the assholes on the ropes. Now is not the time to give up, but rather to press forward, and finish them off. In the war on assholism, we must show no mercy—and take no prisoners. An enema, after all, must be a complete cleansing, or it is not worth much.

Having no real substance to support their claims, the assholes will retreat into the brown fog of propaganda. We must insist that they stick to the facts of their failures. Make them defend their dismal record.

Undoubtedly, they will trot out statistics to support their claims. Do not be deterred. Just quote from Hermione Hunnycutt's famous book, *Lies, Damn Lies, and Public Relations.* "As an expert in public relations, I knew that opinion polls and statistics were always my best friends, because they can be rigged to get any result you want. If someone paid me $50,000 and gave me two weeks, I could prove that most people believe the earth is flat, that we've never been to the moon, and that they actually want to pay more taxes. In the hands of an expert, bullshit not only walks, but also rides a unicycle and dances the tango!"

The burden is ours. Only the decent people in the world can solve this problem, by taking the offensive. One person cannot do it. We must all come together and present a united front.

When we hear people claim there is no truth and everything is relative, we must fight back. We must riddle their argument with holes. If someone tells us it is all right to believe anything you want, we must inquire if it would be okay to come over and hit him? And will it be okay to borrow his car for the next 12 months? Will it be all right when his boss asks him to work for nothing—or when his bank informs him that they believe he has only half of the money he thought he had in his account?

It is not necessary to persuade the asshole he or she is wrong. Just standing up and exposing the truth will alert other decent people that they do not have to be conned and cheated anymore. All we need to do is get the ball rolling. Once it gains momentum, it will grow on its own.

To do this, however, we must be sure to separate facts and opinions clearly in our own minds. We must understand that most things in life are not subject to our whims or fantasies. We must be guided by our clear, rational thought—not the enticements and seductiveness of the asshole sirens.

This third stage is the most dangerous, because the Association knows that the battle of propaganda is the one war they cannot afford to lose. Once the brown fog is lifted, the whole world will be able to see what has been going on. Their little brown tricks won't work anymore.

For this reason, you can expect the bullshit to fly hot and furiously, once the battle has been joined. We must not expect any help from the media—they are a major part of the problem, after all. We must be ready to persevere in the face of the biggest snow job since the start of time.

If we have the persistence, however, we can win. Every denial the press makes will convince more decent people that the media truly is filled with assholes. Every charge of slander the Super Browns make will alert more good folks to the truth of what is actually happening.

Once a certain point of critical mass is reached,

you can expect the whole damn conspiracy to blow up, bullshit and all.

4. We must support decent behavior by example and rhetoric as intensely as possible. At first, this may seem an almost impossible task, especially when you weigh the kind of leadership we have been electing recently. But there is a way!

The secret is to co-opt the goals of assholes and show them dramatically that they can reach them faster, safer, and more successfully if they employ honest, decent means than if they cheat and try to steal from us.

This is actually true; the problem is that no assholes, not even the Super Browns, have ever bothered to think it through and realize the facts of the matter. They have just *assumed* that they had to cheat and steal to get what they wanted.

The goal of the Association is to undermine the values and standards of decent human beings. The genius of this fourth step is that it is a single stroke that can pre-empt this tactic of the asshole, and turn it around. Our goal is to undermine their dependency on cheating, lying, scheming, and bullshit.

• We must show them that they can make more money from honest labor than by thievery—and they get to keep it, too.

• We must show them that people will care for them and help them when life is hard on them if they have treated their friends and relatives with respect and love in the first place—rather than taking advantage of them.

• We must show them that they will feel much better about themselves if they treat others fairly

159

and make truth and honesty their guiding principles.

For eons, decent people have assumed that everyone thought about life and approached it the same way they did. This left an enormous opening for assholes to do their dirty deeds.

Now is the time to close the gap. Decent people have to enunciate and promote their methodology as being more productive and superior to the backstabbing, cheating, double-crossing methods of the asshole.

When a minister berates us for being full of sin, we have to stand up and cry: "Shame! Shame! You are the one who is full of it. Why don't you go out and get an honest job?"

When a politician promises us heaven on earth for just a few billion dollars more, we have to be ready to shout: "Shame! Shame! You are as bankrupt as the country. Try saving us money for a change."

When a professor tries to indoctrinate students in a certain way of thinking, decent people must be prepared to protest: "Shame! Shame! Stop being a shill for asshole propaganda. Challenge us to think, instead of just brainwashing us."

Somehow, we have to convince the assholes that the qualities of the decent life—wisdom, competence, integrity, fair play, and goodwill—are more important than getting a new Porsche or even a promotion. In the same way, we must convince society that the well-being of the nation as a whole is far more important than welfare checks and other entitlements.

In essence, we must make assholes lust for

wisdom, decency, and honesty, even more than they lust for money, sex, and power. We must make it clear that we value decency above everything else. Once that is established beyond a doubt, the assholes will make it their number one goal, too.

They will line up to become decent. They will even lie and cheat and scheme to become decent. But then they will realize that they have been trapped, because the drive for decency will gradually undermine the strength of their dishonesty, scheming, and cheating.

The plan is foolproof—so brilliant that even if you warn the assholes ahead of time what you plan to do, you can still convert them. I have tested and proven this methodology in thousands of cases of recovered assholes.

Whether or not it will work in giving society an enema is up to you—to decent people everywhere. Stand up and be counted. Be proud of your innate decency! Arm yourself with honesty, goodwill, and integrity.

Let the assholes know they are outnumbered, outwitted, and undone.

23
Apocalypse Now

> If there is hell on earth, I know what
> it is now. It is any room with an ass-
> hole in it.
> —*Dr. Crement's Pocket Guide To*
> *Surviving Assholism*

Being a man of integrity, I knew I could not sit back and expect my fellow decent humans to mount the attack on the assholes all by themselves. I knew I had to take a lead in awakening the slumbering majority and stirring it to action.

Little did I know how much I would be stirring up! But who better than me to start the onslaught? Given what I had discovered, I felt it was my duty to step forward. After all, throughout the country, my name was virtually synonymous with assholism. I was known—usually affectionately—as the "asshole doctor," which is no terrible thing to say to a former proctologist. Hundreds of thousands of people had either read my books or were happily recovering from assholism in an ANAL workshop. I knew I could count on this huge base to support me.

So I entered the fray, holding a press conference

to announce that I had come upon evidence that confirmed the existence of the Association, a secret group promoting assholism throughout society. I said that this organization was actively conspiring to undermine the major institutions of society, from government and business to the media and education. I explained that their method of operating was primarily one of confusing the general public through mind control and the distortion of values and ethics.

"Make no mistake about it," I said. "They are out to suck us into poverty, suck us into a dark age of unreason, suck us into fear, into guilt, and into self-loathing. They have pledged to keep on sucking until they have sucked us—and society—to death!"

I took a broad swipe at the whole range of assholism—at how the Super Browns have exploited the women's movement, the racial issue, the gay right's movement, and the abortion debate for their own devious ends. I pointed out the abundance of evidence that they call the shots on how the news is reported through the media. I blew the whistle on their clever scheme to seduce a whole generation through corrupt college professors. And I warned about the insidious weakening of our values and standards—the corrosion of virtue.

"We have substituted propaganda for clear thinking," I said. "And it has gotten to the point where it makes Orwell's *1984* look more like a Disney cartoon."

I had taken pains to be sure the media would not boycott the conference—or consign it to oblivion by failing to report it. As a further precaution, I sent copies of my speech to all members of Congress, the President, his cabinet, major business and media moguls, and other movers and shakers. I packed the audience with my staff and recovered assholes, ready to be interviewed once I had finished. And I contacted everyone I knew in high places in television, to make sure that at least one network would broadcast the entire conference.

The reaction to my announcement was like an explosion in a fireworks factory. The initial response came from the media, who fell all over themselves denying that any of them were controled by assholes—and scoffing at my "paranoid delusions" about an Association.

"If there really were an Association," one editorial ran, "We would have discovered it long ago and exposed it ourselves." The editors apparently did not realize that such blatant arrogance is itself a sign of assholism, and only strengthened my case.

For better or worse, the genie of truth was out of the bottle—and no one could put it back.

But the Association had different plans. Instead of defending themselves—which they couldn't do without admitting that they existed—they simply attacked me.

I had feared that some of the less-committed trainers and leaders in my ANAL program might be vulnerable to asshole exploitation. I was not wrong. Within a week, long articles were appearing in the national press quoting "former associates of Dr. X," who claimed to have evidence of corruption and exploitation within my organization. In just a few days, I was accused of:

Marital infidelity.

Sexual harassment of distaff staffers.

Mail fraud.

Embezzlement.

Tax fraud.

The day after the last charge was made, I got a phone call from the IRS, indicating that they would be auditing me for the last three years. I knew then that if the Association went down, they were going to make sure that it was Armageddon and the Apocalypse all rolled into one.

There was no truth to any of these charges, but they served the purpose of putting me on the defensive. Each day, I had to spend more and more of my time countering the latest attacks. I had to go on *Donahue* to answer a panel of attackers, but I turned that to my advantage in the first five minutes when I asked the audience:

"How many of you consider yourselves to be good, decent people?" The show of hands was unanimous.

"How many of you want to live in a country based on decent values and ethics?" Again the support was unanimous.

"Then let me tell you how to spot the assholes who want to take your enjoyment of life away," I said, and I proceeded to detail the traits of assholism, using the words and acts of my accusers as examples. From then on, whenever one of the accusers tried to attack me, the audience heckled and booed them. Even Phil, a mega-asshole if ever there was one, could not regain control of the audience.

I was also interviewed by another Super Brown, Barbara Halter, on her show *Blindsided*. She insisted that I had made up "all this nonsense" about the Association and demanded that I recant on her show, to purge my soul.

"My soul does not need purging," I rebutted. "But perhaps yours does." I proceeded to play a tape Joe had sent me, in which his colleagues talked candidly about a recent *Blindsided* program.

"Barbara's our gal," one of them exuded. "She's one of the best things that has ever happened to the Association."

Upon hearing this, Barbara started to cry. "You have no right treating me like this," she whimpered. "How low will you stoop to discredit the media? That tape is phony and you know it."

"It is not phony, and I have a sworn affidavit with me to prove it," I said. But Barbara had become petulant and was trying to regain her audience by portraying herself as a victim.

From these skirmishes, the Armageddon got worse. I became accustomed to finding four flat tires on my car when I left my office in the evening. Afraid that the car might even blow up when I started it, I began commuting in a limousine. When the death threats started coming in, I sent my family to Hawaii. I even hired body guards.

But the situation continued to deteriorate. I had difficulty sleeping, and the nightmares began again. I would be chased by rats or sliced by Ninja warriors—or worse. One nightmare involving Hilary Bottum is just too horrible to retell.

While I was awake, I had more and more trouble concentrating. I decided I was suffering from a first-degree case of "brown out."

My staff noticed my problems, of course. My secretary of 20 years even chided me by quoting from my second book, *Assholes Forever,* that no one should ever try to convert or heal the permanent

166

asshole, lest it lead only to total exhaustion. I assured her I was not trying to heal any flaming assholes—I just wanted to throw a wrench in their plans to subvert society. I wanted to alert the decent people of the country to just how serious the asshole conspiracy has become.

"But they are kicking the crap out of you," she said, with concern.

"Let's hope they kick it all out," I joked feebly. She was not amused, but I knew I was taking the right action. If I didn't stand up to the assholes, no one else would, either.

In truth, however, I had not expected the on-slaught to be as fierce as it was. Twice in the first week I suffered mild attacks of food poisoning. Once, I was nearly run over by a car as I crossed the street to get to a television interview. And strange clicking noises began to be audible on the phones at home.

Still, I knew I had to keep the pressure up, until a bandwagon could form that decent people could join. So I agreed to appear on "Meet the Depressed" on national TV. I was confronted there by a panel of professional pessimists who had prepared a long list of shit-trench questions to ask me, and were gleefully looking forward to burying me in my own dung, as one of them put it before the cameras started rolling.

They started out strong: "As a self-admitted ass-hole, in what way do you claim to be different now that you have allegedly recovered from being rude, selfish, mean-spirited, and dishonest?"

"For one thing," I replied, "I no longer twist facts to make them seem different than they are, as you just did. I let the truth speak for itself, without artificially injecting it with bullshit. I was an asshole. I have been recovered for 20 years. I help others recover from being assholes and learn to be decent human beings. I could help you gentlemen, too, if you had the humility to admit that you are, indeed, assholes."

Having been thwarted on the first parry, they tried a different thrust: "How does therapy for recovering assholes differ from other brainwashing techniques?"

"First," I replied, "We must differentiate between brainwashing and brain muddying. Brain washing implies cleansing the mind of former values and beliefs, so that a new script can be implanted. It's what they do to prisoners of war. Brain muddying is what happens when the values and standards you've always cherished are subtly adulterated, so that you don't know what to believe—or do—anymore. It's what assholes have been doing to society.

"My recovery program uses neither one of these techniques. My only technique is what might be called "brain awakening." I ask people to think for themselves and become alert to the menace around them.

"When you fellows sit here week in and week out, spewing forth your pessimistic silliness, you become the ones guilty of brainwashing and brain muddying. You have been responsible for sowing the seeds of despair in thousands of Americans."

Even though I was up to it, the challenge was beginning to wear me down. On one show, I began to yell at the interviewer after he asked if I was hearing voices over light bulbs and getting messages about the Association from the planet Uranus. The little shit deserved to be yelled at, but I knew it made me look bad. I caught myself before doing any real damage, but I could tell by the smile on his face that he knew he had succeeded in rattling me.

The attacks continued. A hastily-called inter-university conference on "Intellectual Liberty in Modern Education" was presented in New York City. Naturally, I was excluded; they limited the panels to the biggest assholes with degrees that they could find. They all proclaimed that free speech and intellectual freedom were not only alive and well but encouraged on campuses everywhere.

I had managed to get several of my supporters into the audience, to record their lies and challenge their distortions. Two were dragged off by conference officials and a third was hit on the head with a chair. A photograph of this incident appeared on the front page of a few papers the next day under such captions as: "Is this what academic freedom means?" and "Is freedom of speech now also a contact sport?"

We learned a lot about the Association in the days that followed. We discovered which newspapers, magazines, and TV stations were under their control, and which were still independent. I rented a half hour of TV time to name names and to ask decent citizens to pressure their local papers and stations to kick out the assholes, if they were on the list.

My initial blitz had shaken loose a few bricks within the Association, too. I began to receive letters and reports in the mail from "former" members of the Association. Frankly, I was surprised they were still alive.

Some of these letters confirmed my suspicions and gave me moral support. Others gave me a glimpse of some of the long-range plans and goals of the Super Browns. In education, for instance, they had planned to encourage free speech as early as kindergarten—and then further dilute government by lowering the voting age to eight. Of course, I knew that their idea of free speech was the right to slander, lie, libel, and distort facts while attacking the opposition.

In religion, the assholes had come up with the scheme to have churches begin promoting "sin-free zones." This did not mean what it seemed to—that the congregation would make a concerted effort to avoid sinning in these zones (work, home, school, or play). Rather, it meant that everyone would be free to sin in the zones. The sin-free zones would be increased every five years until they eventually embraced the entire planet.

The plans for government were more frightening, simply because they were more credible. One of them was the establishment of a Department of Bliss, to monitor and support the good feelings of all citizens. This elaborate system was to be built on the already existing structure of our credit reports. It would enable government to trace and record the acts, thoughts, and feelings of every citizen as they occurred! The interactive potentials of such a setup were downright hellish.

Three weeks into the campaign, I was so tired and fatigued that I had to cut back on my schedule. I plunged myself into finishing this book instead. I figured that it would be the final nail I would have to drive into the coffin I had been preparing for the Association.

One day, as I was working on the book, I fell asleep at my word processor. As I dozed off, I heard faraway voices that said I was doomed.

"I am the Head Brown," a throaty voice rasped. "You and your associates are marked for death. There is no way to avoid our wrath—and you will receive no mercy!"

In the background, I could hear other voices, as though they were dispatching orders to distant members of the Association.

• A psychologist was being ordered to create a new class of victims.

• TV news teams were being directed to step up propaganda about the problems of poverty, drugs, and crime.

• College professors were being ordered to step up the intensity of political correctness on campuses.

• The American flag and the Bill of Rights were to be declared offensive to minorities.

• Democracy was to be lambasted as unfair to the poor.

• Key law enforcement officials were to announce that crime would be recognized as a political statement of protest, as long as it was committed by oppressed minorities. In other words, robbing a liquor store might end up being protected by the Constitution as an act of free speech!

Gee, there's so much to look forward to!

24

A Note From The Publisher

At this point, Dr. Crement's text ends. He collapsed from total exhaustion and is in a private hospital, recovering from his ordeal. The great fatigue he experienced as a result of his heroic efforts sent him to the edge of delirium just before he was hospitalized.

I am happy to report that he is doing well and will be able to return to work soon, although on a reduced scale. The usual author's tour will be delayed until he is strong enough to handle the assholes again.

From the letters we exchanged while the book was in progress, it is clear that Dr. Crement planned to add several more chapters to the book. Apparently, he meant to elaborate on the schemes of the Association for the next few decades. He indicated that the scope and enormity of these plans were so awesome that they were almost unbelievable.

"It's everything you would expect from assholes—

and a whole lot more!" he wrote in one of his letters to me.

When I saw X just before his collapse, he was talking furiously about the inner sanctums of the Association—and how there was a secret enclave of Super Browns in the sub-basement of the Department of Health and Human Services, with secret tunnels to similar rooms under the White House and the Pentagon. Other inner sanctums were to be found in the administration building of UCLA, the Rockefeller Center, and the Teamster's national headquarters.

Since then, X's associates have told me that they had no proof of these claims, and they might just be a product of his fears and fatigue.

It is clear, though, that X does have a lot of information about the sinister workings of the Association—information that he claims would "blow your socks off." I suspect that this is why the Association stepped up the tremendous psychological attack and pressure on him. They wanted him to break. I have no doubt that X was and is the Association's single most deadly threat.

Of course, X would insist that truth itself is the real and enduring danger to all who cheat, lie, and cover up for their personal advantage. In fact, X often told me that "the enemy of the people is the asshole, and the enemy of the asshole is the truth."

I must warn those who read this book that the intense attack against Dr. Crement may have tainted some of his thoughts and writing. I will leave it to each reader to draw his or her own conclusions. Yet, I would not have published this book unless I was firmly convinced in the soundness of this great

173

man's philosophy, goals, and methods. I have total faith in his sincerity and commitment to wipe out all assholism as we know it.

If X were to write the final word here, he would probably warn all of us that we must think deeply about what is going on about us—and to us. There truly is a conspiracy of assholes trying to exploit us and take over our country and culture. We must do something about it—unless we want to hand over our futures, and surrender to the assholes.

And for those who may be plunged into despair or fear by the intensity of Dr. Crement's message, let me close with a quotation from another great book we publish, *The Cry of the Asshole* by Peter Lilly. Mr. Lilly warns us that the most limiting characteristic of assholes is that they stalk and hunt each other.

"This single fact," he writes, "should give all decent humans much comfort. I feel safer knowing that, somewhere out there, the meanest, most devious bunch of assholes is trying to destroy the enemies of human decency and civilization—other assholes like themselves! It's a case of assholes versus assholes, and I don't care who wins.

"When assholes destroy each other, the decent people win."

Now that X has retreated from the scene, there is ample evidence that the assholes have returned to fighting one another. When X returns, I think he will find a brave new world in which decency, wisdom, and goodwill are universally regarded as the essence of truth—and the scourge of assholism.

Want More Copies?

The Asshole Conspiracy makes a wonderful gift for anyone with a nose for what's going on in the world. Additional copies may be purchased at your favorite bookstore, or directly from the publisher.

Two earlier books in the series, *Asshole No More* and *Assholes Forever,* are also available, for the same price.

Orders from the publisher can be made by calling Enthea Press toll free, 1-800-336-7769, and charging your order to MasterCard, VISA, Discover, Diners Club, or American Express. Or send a check for the full amount of your order plus shipping to Enthea Press, P.O. Box 1387, Alpharetta, GA 30239.

The cost of one copy is $11.95 plus $2 for postage. The cost of 10 or more copies is $10 per book plus $3 postage per address. Call for prices on 25 or more copies. The set of all 3 books costs $33 postpaid.

Another book from Enthea Press:

FART PROUDLY

Writings of Benjamin Franklin You Never Read in School
Edited by Carl Japikse

A collection of the satirical and humorous writings of Benjamin Franklin, including his famous essay on farting, "A Letter to the Royal Academy." On sale for $7.95 at bookstores everywhere, or from Enthea Press (add $1.50 shipping).